SHAW'S NAM

JOHN CARN

Benjamin Books
7238 Munsee Lane
Indianapolis, Indiana 46260

All rights reserved.
Copyright © 1984 by John Carn

First Edition
Second Printing: April, 1984
Published by Benjamin Books, 7238 Munsee Lane,
Indianapolis, IN 46260

LIBRARY OF CONGRESS CATALOG CARD NUMBER 84-070275

ISBN 0-916967-00-X

Comment On War by Langston Hughes originally
appeared in *Crisis Magazine,* June, 1940.

Basic cover design by Frieda C. Carn
Silhouette drawings by Louis Latel Butcher

Printed in the USA

*For Charles Edward Jones of Miami,
my closest buddy in Vietnam.*

ACKNOWLEDGMENT

I would like to thank Purdue University English Professor William J. Palmer. He was of invaluable assistance to me during the early stages of this novel.

COMMENT

War is hate.
Peace is love.

Life is everything.
Death is nothing.

John Carn

COMMENT ON WAR

Let us kill off youth.
For the sake of *truth*.

We who are old know what truth is—
Truth is a bundle of vicious lies
Tied together and sterilized—
A war-makers' bait for unwise youth
To kill off each other
For the sake of
Truth.

                        Langston Hughes

PROLOGUE

It was early evening. The month was July and the year, 1967. Jimmy Shaw stepped down the outside stair in front of the two-bedroom house his mother rented. His manner at the moment was carefree. He was eighteen. At that age, being the musician he was, he was called gifted. His long strides took him to the sidewalk. He twisted left and headed for the corner grocery store, three-quarters of a block away at the intersection of two busy streets, 25th and Martindale. Martindale could have been re-named Booker T. Washington Avenue. But the white merchants probably would have opposed. The residents on Martindale were all black.

Inside the grocery 'Mercury' Mike was at work. He was dressed in white tennis-shoes, blue jeans, and a dirty pull-over shirt. He was twenty and one of the neighborhood shoplifters.

If the grocery store owner wasn't aware of Mike's trade, he was now. The owner stood behind the see-through side of the mirror at the end of an aisle watching the regular visitor stuff a package of lunch meat down the front of his pants. The owner was also shaking his head.

Tired of getting ripped-off undoubtedly, he wasted no time dialing the police. He told them that he would be holding a shoplifter. Please hurry.

Only thirty seconds passed before the policemen

stormed the store. Obviously they were in the area. There were two, both white.

The owner was in front of the store now, pointing frantically at Mike. "There he is!"

Mike was facing them, and his big eyes showed fear. He had already served a thirty day jail sentence earlier in the year for selling stolen goods. The judge told him if he saw his baby face again too soon, he would automatically sentence him to six months if it was a similar charge.

The police rapidly approached Mike, their handcuffs and blackjacks out, their .38 caliber handguns secure in their holsters.

"Whacha got, boy," one of the officers said.

Mike backed up. Fear, too, was in his voice. He spoke hurriedly not coolly as usual. "Nothing. I ain't stole nothing."

Backed to the end of the aisle now and the policemen stepping close, Mike struck forward and hit between the policemen like a halfback through a narrow opening. Mike could run. At one time he was an all-state trackman. He had posted 9.8 time in the 100 yard dash.

As Mike sprinted down the long aisle for the front door, a cute, young woman yelled, "Run, Mercury, baby. Ain't nothing in here worth them locking you up for!"

With a grin as he watched Mike speed toward the door, a middle-aged customer said to another, "They'll never catch Mercury Mike. Ol' fast mothafucka should be playing football and running track somewhere."

Shaking his head, the other man grumbled, "If

he'd left that dope alone, he would. The nigga just ain't gonna do right."

Mike was burning now and a step from the open door.

But one of the policemen, apparently, was not to be outdone or embarrassed. Rushing to the door, he unfastened his holster and drew his handgun.

The young woman's yell increased in pitch to a frantic scream. "Don't shoot! Don't shoot, Mercury!"

As if he hadn't expected this or wanted it, the store owner looked terrified when the policeman raised his gun at the door. He pleaded, "Don't shoot! It's not worth it."

The officer ignored all 'don't shoots' as he hurried outside, his gun pointed at the back of Mike.

Mike was 60 yards from the store front, however, and running like he had on the track, straight and swift. But, he probably didn't know the officer's gun was pulled, pointed and cocked.

Jimmy Shaw, now near the store, watched the kids across the street spray water from a hose on each other. It conjured a playful melody.

Then, the command *halt* caught Shaw's ears. He instantly turned his head and saw his football idol being threatened by a policeman's gun. Shaw didn't know what Mercury had done, nor did he care. He just couldn't let him get gunned down.

Mike's eyes were on Shaw, and he ran like a cheetah, still not aware of the life threatening situation.

Shaw looked at him, a very concerned expression on his face, and hollered, "Cut Mercury! Cut now!" Shaw then quickly kneeled, knowing he would be in the policeman's line of fire.

Like a miniature open-hearth furnace, fire shot from the barrel of the officer's precisely aimed weapon.

But Mike had made the cut advised by Shaw just a fraction of a second before the weapon fired.

As the gunshot heartstoppingly echoed through the neighborhood and the bullet zipped menacingly down the sidewalk of Martindale, luckily on a clear path, Mike sped out of sight of the policeman, running between two houses. He had cut sharply. To a Chicago Bear fan, the cut would have brought memories of Gayle Sayers. To the typical Army recruiter, the cut would have made him think that was the kind of man he needed for Vietnam: one who could dodge bullets!

Never would it dawn on the recruiter, particularly one who hadn't been to Vietnam, that Shaw was really the kind of man he needed to fight the war: one who was astute, brave, humane, and loyal.

CHAPTER 1
Fort Lewis

The nightmare was soon to become true—but only part of it, Shaw hoped. Late March, 1968, and Private Jimmy Shaw was in Fort Lewis, Washington, on his way to the war in Vietnam. The nightmare had first occurred eight months earlier, three months before his **greetings** from the draft board came. He had anticipated the letter ever since he forfeited his college deferment by dropping out of Purdue University in May after one semester.

The first nightmare: it came early in the morning. His younger but bigger brother, Joey, who slept in the same little room, woke him from it.

"Jimmy, Jimmy!" Joey yelled hysterically. Then with both hands he grabbed Jimmy by the shoulder and yanked his long, thin, 5 foot-11 inch, 145 pound frame. As Jimmy opened his dark brown eyes, Joey asked, "What's wrong? You okay?"

Jimmy wiped his sweaty, brown face with the palm of his hand. He looked at Joey and answered as calm as if everything was under control, "Yeah. What's the problem?"

"You were moaning and saying, 'Why me, why me'. I thought something was wrong."

"Just a bad dream. But thanks. Go on back to sleep."

Joey took half a step back and flopped into his twin bed.

Jimmy was now nineteen, and he didn't want Joey, his sixteen-year-old brother, to be ashamed of him for having a nightmare about the war that they always watched on the news for the action.

Shaw had been dreaming that he was a soldier in Vietnam. The scenery was like a shot he had seen in *National Geographic*—a rice paddy wet with water and green with the two foot tall crop, bordered by a lush tree line. He was a sergeant on patrol with his squad when he spotted three Viet Cong soldiers. The VC, wearing green, pajama-like clothing, were crawling toward the palm trees like snakes ducking a mongoose. Seventy-five yards separated the squad and the VC.

Shaw whispered to the machine gunner and pointed to the VCs' movement.

The machine gunner opened fire, the M-60 rattling on his hip, *Rat-tat-tat-tat . . .,* spitting out ten rounds a second, every fifth round a fiery red tracer. The burst of fire lasted five seconds as two of the targets darted like scared jackrabbits into the jungle of trees, but the other laid motionless in the paddy, blood spurting from its head.

Raising his hand and waving it forward, Shaw motioned his squad to pursue.

The entire squad advanced at double-time.

Shaw was out front when he tripped over a wire and fell. Every muscle in his body tightened because of what he feared next. "Booby trap!" he hollered in an unusually high pitched voice.

Boom! the explosion, as he had feared. Then he felt fragments of metal rip and pierce his body as he went airborne three feet.

He hit the ground and blacked-out.

When he opened his eyes, all he saw was a swaying, gray sky. He quickly realized that he was on a stretcher.

His lower right arm burned, and he moaned in pain. He lifted his head slightly and shifted his eyes down to the painful area. At first glance all he saw was gauze and tape. An instant later he realized that he had no hand. He closed his eyes, and after a moment he moaned in sorrow, "Why me, why me." The thought of not being able to play the piano again—the instrument he had loved since his father taught him the basics thirteen years before—stabbed at him as he passed out.

He didn't remember anything else but Joey's frantic, sweet voice bringing him back to reality. Thank god, it was only a nightmare, he thought!

Shaw stood outside one of the frame, transit barracks at Fort Lewis as he remembered that nightmare. He knew that becoming a soldier in Vietnam would soon be a reality. But in spite of his dream, he wasn't particularly frightened by the thought of going to Nam.

Shaw really didn't know why his country was fighting in Vietnam. And he couldn't have cared less. From all he had learned in high school about the war, he concluded that it was a mistake. But he knew why he was going, because he had to go or else go to jail, just like he had had to register with the Selective Service.

He had a plan for when he got to Vietnam, however, to come back alive and intact. But even though he felt he could survive, he really didn't want to chance it. He had briefly considered other alternatives. One was to refuse to obey orders and be sent to the stockade to work hard labor in the daytime and be confined to an 8 by 8 cell at night for probably twice as long as a tour of duty in Vietnam, with a dishonorable discharge following. However, twenty-four months in the stockade and a discharge that would probably prevent him from securing a decent job (paying more than minimum wage) for the rest of his life were too staggering for him to face. Another alternative was simply to desert, to go underground in the States, or become a citizen in another country like Canada. But he knew either course would take money—something neither he nor his mother (nor father if he could locate him) had.

Standing in the chilly air at Ft. Lewis, Shaw watched and listened. It was daylight. Incoming and outgoing soldiers milled around the barracks waiting to be processed either home or out of the country. Some smoked cigarette after cigarette; others sipped from wine and whiskey bottles that they normally kept hidden under their field jackets.

Soldiers returning from Vietnam wore the gold, red and green pin-striped campaign ribbon over their left shirt pocket. Some said little or nothing. Most overflowed with conversation. One lanky veteran answered the questions of an inquisitive greenhorn who, like Shaw, wore no overseas ribbons under his open field jacket.

"I've finished my twelve months in hell," the vet said, exhaling a deep breath. "I wish you all the luck in the world!" He paused and Shaw read D'Angelo printed across the name plate over his right shirt pocket. The vet stood straight and proud like an Olympic athlete being awarded the gold medal. His face was suntanned and roughened by a mild, active case of acne. Shaw thought D'Angelo looked at least five years older than him. D'Angelo weighed as much as Shaw, but was an inch-and-a-half taller. Bristles of closecut, dark brown hair stood on his head except where his dark green garrison cap covered it. Since troops weren't allowed to take dress green suit-uniforms to Vietnam, D'Angelo was wearing his short sleeve, khaki uniform. But because it was a damp, cool day at Ft. Lewis, Shaw wondered why the vet wasn't wearing a field jacket like most of the other soldiers.

D'Angelo continued, "All I can say is don't get assigned to the Central Highlands. They're fighting like mad around there. And take good care of your M-16. Clean it. Keep it with you all the time, kid."

Unexpectedly, the young soldier complained, " 'Kid!' You're trying to sound like you're old enough to be my dad. You're not too much older than me. I'm eighteen. What about you?"

The veteran's brown eyebrows suddenly arched more. "I'm twenty-two, kid! And when you do a year in the Nam, then I'll say 'man!' " The vet turned and walked away like an un-rejoicing boxer from a downed opponent. He walked in Jimmy Shaw's direction, leaving the eighteen year old standing quiet and pale-faced.

Shaw admired D'Angelo, though not entirely for his words and actions but mostly for the story that the stripes, the campaign ribbons, and the badges on his uniform told. D'Angelo's uniform fit like it was tailor made. Three yellow rank stripes were sewn across each khaki colored sleeve. Campaign ribbons above his left shirt pocket indicated that he had served in Germany, too. He wore the purple heart, the expert rifleman badge, the paratrooper badge, and the combat infantry badge. Shaw looked at his shoulder patch to see what unit he had been with in Vietnam. Airborne, the 173rd, it designated. Shaw knew that the 173rd had months earlier whipped a well-trained, well-equipped North Vietnamese battalion around Dak To in the Central Highlands. The battle had received considerable attention from the news media and considerable praise from the Army generals.

Then Shaw glanced down at D'Angelo's knob-toed paratrooper boots. Shaw had great admiration for paratroopers. He wasn't sure if it was because of the rugged training they endured or because they were the only soldiers allowed to wear the knob toe boots. The knob toe reminded him of the elegant ghetto shoe, the Stacy Adam.

From the first day of basic training, Shaw had wanted to be a paratrooper. But he didn't volunteer for jump school because he knew his chances of going to Vietnam would be greater as a paratrooper. He took basic at Ft. Campbell, Kentucky. And at the time he was there, the entire 101st Airborne Division was preparing to ship out to Vietnam. As far as he knew, there were only two other airborne units, the 173rd and the 82nd, and the 173rd was already in Vietnam. He had read in the newspaper how they beat the hell out of the North Vietnamese while sustaining heavy casualties.

Another reason he didn't sign up for jump school was because he had seen first hand how thuggish many of the paratroopers were. But their foul play didn't scare Shaw; it disgusted him. During his fourth week of basic training, some of the more disciplined trainees—those with consistently close shaven faces, shined boots, and clean, starched fatigues—were given off-base privileges. Shaw's white bunkmate, Private Moores, had earned the privilege and decided to go to the city, Clarksville. He left by taxi Friday evening only to return in an ambulance that night.

Shaw talked to him the next day at the infirmary

where he was recovering from a slight concussion. "What happened?"

"A couple of colored paratroopers mugged and robbed me."

Shaw believed that Moores used the word 'colored' as if to suggest the attack had been racially motivated; but, being black, Shaw did not want to accept that. He felt the paratroopers simply needed money. Deep in his mind, though, he knew the incident had some racial overtones. He doubted if the two black paratroopers would have viciously assaulted a black for only a few Army dollars.

And there was another incident involving airborne troops. One October evening Shaw heard two blacks arguing vehemently. They were paratroopers. It seemed four out of every ten paratroopers at Ft. Campbell were black. These two stared at each other like boxers before round one. Just five feet of thin air was between them.

Because Shaw had grown up in one of the toughest ghettos on the eastside of Indianapolis, he knew that this kind of heated argument usually erupted into a wicked fist fight. And he didn't want whites, like his bunkmate, generalizing that blacks were animals: vicious and ruthless.

Shaw thought that he could prevent the imminent clash. One paratrooper was three inches shorter and twenty-five pounds lighter than the other. Still, the smaller one was heavier than Shaw, and verbally, he was the most aggressive. Slowly, Shaw took short steps toward them.

The two shifted their eyes when Shaw stopped near them. Although their attention was diverted only momentarily, it was enough to cool them. The larger trooper stepped back and said, "Forget it, man."

The smaller trooper backed up and said, "All right."

The less aggressive one walked away first.

Shaw shook his head, thinking, *A close call for the big dude.* The little fellow had an equalizer—a shiny, three-inch blade pocket knife—in his hand, hidden behind his thigh. Shaw had the feeling, though, that the big fellow knew.

After that incident Shaw figured the surroundings in airborne units were practically no different from the one he grew up in, the kind he had been trying to get away from for so long!

Other veterans followed after Sergeant D'Angelo left, but the scenes and conversations were basically the same. Shaw watched and listened for another half-hour, then yawned. There was nothing else he wanted to do except take a nap and then leave Ft. Lewis. It had become boring. His reluctance to go to Vietnam faded, too, and he knew that in a few hours he would be on his way.

CHAPTER 2
Cam Ranh Bay

From the time, fifteen hours ago, when Shaw had boarded the commercial airliner at the Seattle-Tacoma Airport, he had been in the company of two hundred-fifty other uniformed soldiers. There were also stewardesses and civilians. The twenty civilians, however, had left the plane in Hawaii, the first intermediate stop.

"To fly two hours more," one of the stewardesses said as she handed Shaw the cognac and Coke that he had ordered. Shaw noted the awkward way she spoke. She and five other stewardesses had not been on the plane long, four hours; the crew had changed in Japan, the second intermediate stop. She was as thin as a fashion model, and she stood at least half a foot shorter than most. Her hair was pure black and straight, extending down the back of her pastel blue suit-uniform to the lower part of her shoulder blades. Her perfume smelled as fresh as blooming flowers and unlike any fragrance Shaw had smelled in the States. She was Oriental. He figured that she was Japanese only because she had boarded the plane there. He could never really distinguish one Oriental nationality from another, because, in Indianapolis, he had seen very few people of those races; and the few he had seen were simply referred to as Orientals, not Japanese-Americans or Chinese-Americans.

After the flight Shaw was sure that the stewardess would be speaking English more naturally; she got a lot of practice talking to soldiers trying to hit on her. He had overheard a guy in back of him tell her that she looked good. A guy further back asked her for a mailing address. And a brother across the aisle told her that she was fine! She had talked with each one for a minute or two as if she had heard it all before.

About an hour after the stewardess gave Shaw the cognac and Coke, the pilot began announcing something over the PA. Conversation in the cabin suddenly folded. "We," he began his next sentence, "are about to make our descent. Please be seated and fasten your seat belts. We will be arriving in the Republic of South Vietnam in approximately forty-five minutes. The time there is 12:10, and the temperature is 78 degrees in Cam Ranh Bay, where we will be landing. Thanks and best of wishes."

A snow job. This republic stuff and 80 degree weather; it was freezing in Japan. It was almost like when Shaw was reluctant to let the nurse inject a needle in his arm for his first childhood inoculation. She said that it wouldn't hurt, so he stopped crying, reassured that everything would be painless. He remembered that it felt like being poked hard in the arm with the heavy end of a baseball bat.

As soon as the hum of the PA faded, a soldier blurted, "The pilot sounds like he's gonna be landing us in a tropical paradise!"

Another laughed, "Palm trees, bikinis and everything!"

The cabin soon buzzed with conversation again. However, Shaw and a few other soldiers sat quiet. Shaw took the pair of horn-rimmed, clear lens glasses from his shirt pocket and placed them on his face. Even though he was as nearsighted as a watchmaker, he rarely wore them. He had developed a complex about being called four-eyed and treated like an outsider when he first wore them as a twelve-year-old.

Shaw turned his head and stared out the cabin window. The light blue sky was radiantly lit, brighter than any he had ever seen. He knew that it was because he was closer to the equator than he had ever been before. *Maybe it is 78 degrees, like the pilot said.*

Once the plane flew under the low set, patchy cloud cover, the darker blue of the sea came into view. Shaw glanced out the window, looking for land. At each glance the view of the sea narrowed. After his seventh glance—presto—there it was: Vietnam! The sandy brown coastline contrasted with the green and brown inland. A purplish mountain stood tall in the background.

As the plane dipped, Shaw could see the hundreds of people swimming near the coastline in the wavy, blue water and lying on the shore suntanning. Further in, the metal roofs of housing reflected the sunlight. And the foliage was thick and green except where brown dirt roads cut and wound through it. The main road ran for nearly two miles to the base of the mountain range and continued in a zig-zag to the top of the highest mountain, at 2,500 feet. There, antenna towers and a disk were barely visible through the purplish haze.

Shaw was surprised at the scenes on the ground. He had expected the war would have had people so preoccupied with survival that recreation like swimming would be almost non-existent. He had expected, too, to see some evidence of battles: some ruins or smoldering bomb craters.

A smirk appeared on Shaw's face. He sat back and

took a deep breath. *I wonder if I can get some pictures and souvenirs to send home to Joey. I wonder if a lot of Vietnamese speak English?* He felt like a tourist.

The plane flew in low, landing gear down. It bounced slightly as it hit the paved runway. Then it steadied, slowed and rolled to a stop.

Dark blue buses and freight vehicles started from the terminal, half a mile down the runway. In one minute they reached the plane. Air Force drivers, who wore green, tropical fatigues, parked their vehicles by the plane.

The door to the plane opened, and soldiers curiously began stepping out into the Nam. Heads swung left and right. Eyes moved all around.

Shaw retrieved his duffle bag from one of the flat bed, freight vehicles.

An airman first class wearing dark glasses stood between the line of blue buses and freight vehicles. "On here," he called out, pointing to the first bus.

With their duffle bags on their shoulders, Shaw and some of the others made double time to the bus. Shaw stepped on and found a seat in the front, next to the window. He wanted to take in as much of the country as he could. It fascinated him, the vegetation, the mountains, the warm weather in late March—all things that he had never experienced in Indianapolis.

The dark glasses the airman was wearing caused Shaw to think of the pair that he had in his duffle bag. His sunglasses contained prescription lenses. The Army had made them. Before then he had never owned a pair of prescription sunglasses because he couldn't afford them. He thought, with the sky being so bright in Vietnam, that was good enough reason to wear them all the time. He took the key ring out of his pocket and unlocked the duffle bag. He removed some white underwear and towels before he found the sunglasses. He took the clear lens glasses from his perspiring face and placed them in the soft case, put the sunglasses on, then repacked the duffle bag.

As soon as the bus loaded full, the airman drove off. Once off the airstrip, the bus rolled along a dirt road past wooden barracks within the compound. All the buildings' floors were elevated two or three feet because during monsoon season heavy rains usually flooded the low land. The double-slanted roofs were constructed of sheets of aluminum, with sandbags weighting down sections of the roof. The monsoon season also brought typhoons. As the bus rolled steadily at thirty miles-an-hour, a dark green jeep zipped around it. Two soldiers rode in the open vehicle. They wore helmets and carried rifles.

We are in a war, then. Shaw showed no emotions with his thought.

The bus stopped after a mile-and-a-half run. "This is where you guys get off," the driver said. "It's your Army's incoming processing company." The driver had stopped and parked just inside the front gate of the Army complex.

All thirty-two soldiers unloaded, and almost as soon as the last man stepped off the bus, someone hollered. "Attention!"

Everyone instinctively stopped what he was doing, stood straight up, faced the helmet-wearing officer and saluted.

As a means of camouflage, the officer's helmet was

fully covered with a cloth shaded green and dapped with brown and black splotches. He stood within ten feet of the group of soldiers, his face smooth and without a trace of hair. His bright, blue eyes were wide open as they shifted from one end of the staggered rank to the other. His youthful face and small stature made him look like a kid.

Instead of a shiny silver or gold plated rank bar pinned to the lapel of his camouflage fatigues, a black fabric bar was sewn there. Officers as well as enlisted men had learned from basic training that in hostile places like Vietnam, reflective surfaces could cost someone his life. Sewn on the other lapel was a narrow patch with two crossed rifles.

After looking over the group several times, the young infantry officer finally saluted.

The group dropped their hands.

"Welcome to Vietnam, soldiers. I'm Lieutenant Sargent."

One of the soldiers began snickering.

Wasting no time, the lieutenant glanced down the rank. He spotted the culprit. "Soldier!" he said with intensity.

"Yes sir," the private returned, now looking at the ground.

"What were you laughing at?"

"Auh, auh, I really don't know, sir."

"You're a liar, soldier! We both know what it was. It was the combination of my rank and name, wasn't it? I'm very conscious of that. I've had people laugh before. It's a good thing for you that this didn't happen in the States. I'd have you doing a hundred push-ups, at least. But in the Nam it's a little different." He glanced over the entire rank. "I try not to alienate anyone because I know our success will depend upon how well we work together." Then he eyed the private again. "Think about that next time you decide to laugh at someone."

"As all of you should know," the lieutenant continued with less emotion, "we're in Cam Ranh Bay. If it appears peaceful here, that's because it's like being in the rear; if there is such a thing fighting guerrillas. Once you get in the bush, you'll definitely know there's a war going on."

He paused for a moment, then returned, "Your stay here will probably be brief. All of you will be assigned to one of those barracks in front of you." The first barrack was fifty feet from them. "We expect you to remain in or around your assigned barrack so that you can be located when the time comes. And one other thing: get out of those khaki uniforms."

Shaw had been assigned to Delta barrack. The first thing he did was take a nap. He simply chose an empty cot, enclosed, like the others, in a mosquito net. Eight cots were on each side of the middle aisle, and at the foot of some of the cots duffle bags sat on the plywood floor.

When Shaw awoke, he was hungry and figured it was dinner time. He walked to the head, in a separate building. There, he leaked and washed his hands. The flushing toilets and hot running water were a pleasant surprise; he had always been told the Nam was a primitive place. He decided that he would take a shower after dinner and change to one of the green, tropical, fatigue uniforms that he had been issued in the States after receiving orders for Vietnam. The fatigues were lighter in weight and looser in fit than the regular ones. Most men called them jungle utilities. Shaw left the head, following a couple of guys whom he had overheard saying that they were going to dinner.

Shaw could smell the aroma of roast beef as he neared the mess hall, and he could see a line of soldiers waiting to be served. He counted eighteen as he approached the line. In a matter of seconds he and the two soldiers that he had followed made it twenty-one.

The guy in front of Shaw turned around and eyed him.

Shaw ignored the guy by looking over his shoulder at the mess hall. *Maybe he knows I followed them.* Shaw had lagged behind them only about twenty feet for that stretch of two stateside blocks.

"Where you from, blood?" the guy asked Shaw.

Surprised, Shaw fixed his eyes on the guy and said, "Indianapolis, my man." He had been expecting to hear something like, 'What you been following us for?' particularly from a guy whose face was nearly as dark as ebony and whose thick, veined neck sat on a weightlifter's frame. The guy stood just as tall as Shaw.

"What about you?" Shaw asked, gently, like the way he'd strike the keys of the piano on a particular chord, calling for the soloist to play soft and easy.

"I'm from Cleveland," he said slowly. "So you from Naptown. There's two other brothers from Naptown in Echo."

He was speaking of Echo barrack, Shaw gathered; it was next to his. "Yeah?" His eyes widened under his dark glasses. "What's their names?"

The guy shut his eyes and leaned his head backward. After a moment he opened his eyes and replied, "That's funny, I know their names, but cain't remember now."

The other guy, who hadn't said anything, turned

around toward his buddy and interjected, "Jackson and Pope."

"Aw, yeah. Thanks Clem," the guy acknowledged as he still faced Shaw.

Clem turned back around toward the mess hall.

"I tell you what," the guy continued, talking to Shaw, "I stay in Echo, too. Come on over after chow, and I'll turn you on to them. Where you staying at now?"

"Delta."

"All right! Right next to us. I'm Myers, man," the guy said even though his last name was printed in black lettering just above his left shirt pocket. He reached out to shake Shaw's hand.

Shaw reached out his own.

When their hands touched, Myers looked down at them and commented, "Naw, blood. Brothers don't shake hands like that in the Nam. I had to learn, too. So don't feel bad." Myers raised his head and said, "You see I been 'round here a week waiting on my orders, but I been learning all the time. So anyway you look at it, I cain't do no more than 358 days in the bush."

Shaw kind of suspected that Myers was going to take him on a tangent.

With both hands Myers grasped his trousers at the belt, lifted and twisted them, then said, "Aw, yeah, about the handshake. I curl my four fingers 'round your four fingers."

They executed, Myers saying, "And the thumbs go on top, you dig?"

"Yeah," Shaw answered, grinning. "I'm Jimmy Shaw, and glad to meet you Myers. What's your first name?"

Myers cocked his head to the side, looked at Shaw

somewhat strangely, as if he had been offended. Suddenly he began smiling.

"That's when Shaw noticed the gold crown on one of his upper, pure white, front teeth.

"It's Ortho," he said, still smiling. Then as quick as a caution light, his smile disappeared. "Call me Myers, though."

The three of them hardly said anything else until they entered the mess hall.

The mess hall was filled with enough wooden bench tables to feed a couple of platoons; and, like all Army mess halls, it was clean. The steam table was buffed to a gloss. The floor was being swept by a Vietnamese porter.

As Shaw moved through the line, he turned his head every fourth step or so and eyed the porter, a little man in his late twenties whose long, black hair fell over his ears and rounded at the base of his neck. His skin was more tan than yellow, and he had those Oriental eyes.

Once Clem, Myers, and Shaw got their food and stepped away from the line, Myers turned around and said, "Sit with us."

Shaw stared at him momentarily. *What else did you think I was going to do!* Then he simply returned, "That's a good idea." He followed them to an empty rectangular bench table on the far side of the mess hall. The table was large enough to seat six persons.

The roast beef was tender, Shaw thought as he started eating. But the mashed potatoes tasted like they had been rehydrated with too much water. The whole kernel corn had a canned taste. And the milk didn't taste dariy fresh, but more like a flat powdered milk. The rolls were warm and tasted fresh, though.

Shaw drank some cold water and noticed Myers looking across the mess hall.

Myers then attempted to holler at someone; but instead, he accidentally spit bits of food on Clem's tray.

Clem sat unmoved as he just easily laid down his fork.

Shaw was glad now that he had chosen to sit next to Myers.

"My fault, Clem," Myers apologized while wiping an area on the table with a paper napkin. "Go get you another plate."

Clem spoke. "It's all right. I wasn't too hungry. I don't want anymore."

Myers raised his head and finally hollered, "Hey y'all!"

Nearly everyone in the mess hall, for an instant, turned toward that table.

Two guys in the serving line waved at Myers, and one yelled, "Hold those seats!"

Myers and Shaw resumed eating.

And in minutes, the two guys came and sat down at the table. "You get any orders yet?" the husky one asked, looking at Myers. The big guy had a handsome face. His skin was smooth, light brown like the sand and accented by a thin, brown mustache. The kinky, half inch-long hair around his green fatigue cap was hazel. His nose was lean and angular like the typical Caucasian's. His lips were curved and full like the typical Negro's.

Myers hesitated a second as he swallowed his food. Then he replied, "Not yet. Maybe they'll slip up and let me stay here for a year." His teeth gleemed as he grinned.

"Ha, haa," the husky guy laughed loud. He removed and tucked his fatigue cap inside the belt holding his trousers. "Then they gonna realize the mistake and have your black ass do a year in the worst part of the country for not telling 'em you hadn't been assigned anywhere."

"Bullshit! I'm going home in 358 days, regardless." Myers paused, glanced at Shaw and said, "Hey," as if forgetting something. He then looked across the table at the two who had just sat down. "Pope and Jackson, here's one of your homeboys, brother Shaw."

They looked at Shaw and broke into smiles. The husky guy spoke. "I'm Larry." Pope was printed across his namestrip. He reached out his hand across the table.

Shaw reached out his. Shaw's basic brown skin appeared three or four shades darker than Pope's.

They shook hands, thumbs on top, like Myers had taught Shaw.

"I'm Jimmy, man."

When they released hands, the other guy spoke. "And I'm Dean Jackson." Jackson's face resembled Shaw's: the heavy, black eyebrows, the moderately broad nose, the slightly pimpled cheeks, and the semi-full lips. However, noticeably different were their hair and skin tone. Both had black hair, but Jackson's was wavy; Shaw's was kinky. Shaw's was cut short, less than a quarter inch, side and top. Jackson's was twice that length on the sides and three times longer on the top. Shaw had a fuzz-like mustache that, from infrequent shaving, ended at the corners of his lips. Jackson could grow no appreciable amount of hair on his face, and his complexion was a couple of shades brighter than Shaw's.

"What side of town you from?" Jackson asked as he and Shaw shook hands across the table.

"Eastside."

"Yeah," Jackson nodded, wide-eyed. "You went to Tech, then?"

"Naw, Shortridge. I could have went to Tech, but I thought it was too big."

"And raggedy!" Pope interrupted, giggling and looking at Jackson. "Dean, you know I ain't got nothing nice to say about your school."

"That's right," Jackson said, grinning. "You went to jive time Shortridge, too." The two schools were major sports rivals, particularly in basketball.

Shaw instantly shifted his widened eyes onto Pope. "What year did you come out?"

" '67."

"I came out in '66. I'm surprised I don't know you."

"I've seen you around, man. I thought I had when I first sat down."

Then it dawned on Shaw. "Hey, man, shit, you just graduated in June. What you doing over here?"

Responding to Shaw's first statement, Pope said, "Nine months ago." He sounded serious for the first time as the grin on his face evaporated. "But you see, I volunteered right after graduation. So I guess the Army figured they could do what they wanted with a fool like me. And I'm not the only guy who has volunteered and later said he felt like a fool for having signed up for a year longer than if he had just waited and gotten drafted. But the thing was, a volunteer was supposed to be guaranteed the MOS of his choice if he was qualified.

A frown developed on Pope's now reddened face. "Yeah, the Army fucked me around. I signed up for radar repair school. I figured I could learn a skill and still not have to worry about fighting even if I did get assigned to Vietnam. But what happened was I couldn't get through the course, not enough math in high school.

And after I flunked out they sent me to infantry school instead of sending me back through the course. So here I am," he said with a sneer, "a mothafuckin groundpounder, not a repairman."

Everyone at the table sat stunned—not a word was spoken, not an eye moved off Pope.

Then like a psychiatrist snapping his finger to bring a group out of hypnotism, Pope said, "It ain't that bad, y'all." A tinge of humor was in his voice.

Relieved, the others burst into laughter and began eating.

When Myers finished, he and Clem left the mess hall. Shaw, Pope and Jackson stayed and talked.

"Let's have a reunion when we get back to Nap. Let's just party: get high, get some broads and freak off," Pope said, looking at Jackson and then Shaw. "When did you get here?"

"This afternoon," Shaw answered.

"Me and Dean been here almost two days."

"Can you believe," Jackson added, "we even flew over here on the same plane."

Behind the dark glasses Shaw shifted his eyes to Jackson. "I wonder if y'all 'll get assigned to the same place?"

"Maybe," Jackson said. "But we got different MOSs."

Pope spoke. "Since we all came over around the same time, we might leave on the same day and same plane, but if we don't let's have that reunion sometimes during our 30 day leave." He took a pen from his shirt pocket. On a paper napkin he jotted down some information. Then he handed the napkin to Shaw. "Here's my mother's address and phone number. That's where I'll be staying. Dean already has it. Now why don't you turn us on to your address and number?"

"Sure," Shaw replied with a broad smile. He borrowed Pope's pen and jotted down the information on two napkins. Then he handed Pope one of the napkins and Jackson the other.

The next morning, only minutes after the reveille bugle sounded off through the PA, Shaw was awakened by the shaking of his bed. He opened his eyes and saw a burly uniformed body. Shaw reached for his glasses in the black, vinyl case next to his pillow. He fumbled around with the case for a moment before he finally got the dark glasses out. He tried to set them squarely on his face, but he quickly realized one of the stems was bent. He left them lop-sided. His eyes instantly focused sharply on the upper sleeve of the person now shaking the bed next to him. He saw the stripes of a staff sergeant, three black stripes with a rocker attached underneath.

After awakening everyone in the barrack, the staff sergeant started calling out names. "Crowfoot, Aims, Shaw, Rodriguez, T. C. Jones, and Henson." His voice was loud, deep, and clear. "After breakfast, those six will report outside the orderly room. Make it 0800 sharp." He repeated everything, once.

Shaw was sure his orders had been cut. He was curious to know where he had been assigned. But he was not anxious to leave the secure confines of Cam Ranh Bay. The only disturbance he had seen was drunk soldiers arguing about something.

At 0800 Shaw and five other privates gathered in front of the orderly room. The sun shined down on their faces.

When the door squeaked open, a couple of guys stooped and squinted, looking at the doorway. Then one of them hollered, "Attention." All the men closed their legs and stood straight at attention.

After a brief moment, Lieutenant Sargent fully emerged from the barrack which had Company Orderlyroom painted across its door.

Just as the six enlisted men brought up their right hand to salute, the lieutenant said, "At ease."

The men reverted to standing loose.

"You six men will be flying to Dong Ha this morning."

"Where is that, sir?" the guy standing next to Shaw asked. The voice sounded polite and studious.

Shaw turned his head and glanced at the tall, white guy who was wearing thick glasses.

"It's about 300 miles north of here, in the northern sector of the country," the lieutenant answered, glancing at all the soldiers. "You will be assigned to your unit from there. There's a C-130 taking off from the airfield at 10:40. You will be on that flight with your gear and these papers." He lifted a handful of 8½ by 11 inch papers that were off white and typed in black. "By the way, all you men are PFCs now."

The guy standing next to Shaw spoke again. "Sir, if you don't mind my asking, is this an automatic promotion or did we earn it?"

The lieutenant hesitated a second as he stared at the guy. A sneer was on the lieutenant's baby face. Then he half cracked a smile and said, "We know you'll earn it here." The smile faded almost instantly. "You might say that as soon as a private comes into the country, we advance him to PFC. We know he deserves it."

"What you're saying in effect is an euphemism for not actually earning a promotion, sir."

Shaw gritted his teeth, and kept his thoughts to himself. *Damn, he talks too much, and he's one of those dudes who puts too much into principles. He might blow this advancement for the rest of us. I'd like to tell him to shut up!*

The lightweight at the end of the rank, Rodriguez printed over his shirt pocket, turned his head and stared down the rank at the tall, white guy named Henson. He spoke with volume. "Earn it or not, man. We got promoted. That's fifteen more dollars a month. Now let the lieutenant talk, so we can get this shit over with, man."

The group broke into a light laugh and nodded with approval.

Lieutenant Sargent stepped forward. With one hand he partially covered the smirk on his face. With the other hand he gave each soldier a set of papers. "Buses leave here for the airfield on every hour and half hour during this time of day," he told the group as he reached the last man.

After the lieutenant released them, Shaw trotted to Delta. He wanted to re-pack his duffle bag and have some time to chat with Myers, Pope, and Jackson before he left.

Once inside the barrack, Shaw opened the bag and stuffed in his comb, toothbrush, toothpaste, soap, washcloth, towel and paperback book, *Native Son*. He folded and placed the set of orders in one of the lower shirt pockets on his tropical fatigues. Then he shouldered the forty pound bag, staggered a step, gained his balance, and walked out of the barrack.

As soon as Shaw stepped in Echo, he saw Myers, whose back was toward him. "What's going on!" Shaw opened, stepping forward.

Myers pivoted his sturdy body. His teeth gleamed as usual with his broad grin. "Hey, brother Shaw! What it be like!"

When Shaw got close, Myers extended his hand.

Shaw un-shouldered his duffle bag a few feet from Myers, dropping it to the floor. Then firmly he grasped Myers' hand and shook it.

"You must be leaving?" Myers quizzed.

"Yeah," Shaw returned, his tone flat, "going up to Dong Ha this morning. You know anything about the place?"

"Not really."

"What about your orders?"

Myers grinned. "Haven't heard a thing yet."

Shaw glanced left, right, then over Myers' shoulder. "Where's Pope and Jackson?"

"They split. Didn't they tell ya?"

"Naw." The loudness of his voice increased a notch. "When did they leave?"

"Right after breakfast. Both got assigned to the 1st Air Cav. They went to An Khe. I think that's the Cav's home base."

"What area of the country is that in?"

"Almost in the center—Central Highlands."

Shaw's heart thumped. He feared the worst because of what he knew about the Highlands. The tone of his voice flattened even more. "Well okay, brother Myers. I'm gonna cut out."

"All right then," Myers returned, his face straight, "and may God be with you."

Shaw's eyebrows raised a bit. What Myers said kind of surprised him. He had never conceived that Myers was reverend because he hadn't seen anyone in the church with as much street character as him. At home Shaw had attended Bethel Baptist Church at least one Sunday a month ever since his mother had had him baptized at seven.

They shook hands again, and Shaw said, "And God bless you."

Shaw then went back to Delta and decided to lie down for ten minutes or so. He leaned his duffle bag against the cross support at the foot of the cot. The thin mattress gave a little as he sat down and began untying his jungle boots. The boots were made of green nylon except where black leather covered the lacing area, toes, and heels. The soles and under heels were of black rubber. All in all the boots were more suitable to the wet, hot climate of Vietnam than were the regular, all leather, black boots.

In minutes sleep came and his nightmare returned.

He awoke at the trip wire, yet he wasn't distressed as he had been. Instead, he worried about how long he had slept.

Across the barrack a guy napping had a wristwatch on his arm.

"Hey," Shaw hollered. "Hey, man!"

The guy stubbornly lifted his eyelids, looked in the direction of Shaw, and answered, "Yeah?"

"What time you got?"

Holding up his wrist, "9:55," he read.

Shaw jumped out of the bunk, pulled on his boots and slung the duffle bag over his shoulder. He ran out of the barrack and continued for a quarter mile to the bus loading point.

The on-the-hour bus was still there.

In the airfield terminal Shaw gave the airman behind the counter a copy of his orders. Compared to a commerical terminal, the military terminal was relatively small; one hundred people could pack it. It only had three counters.

The airman turned away from Shaw and pointed out the window to a large cargo plane painted in a pattern and colors similar to the helmet covers. "You don't have much time before that C-130 takes off."

"Thanks. I'll catch it." The terminal was nearly full with soldiers and airmen. Shaw squeezed his way out and ran the sixty yards to the plane. He showed one of the airmen standing at the rear of the prop aircraft his papers.

"Hurry and get on board," the one said, barely glancing at the orders.

The plane's wide, rear door touched the paved airstrip. It served as a loading ramp. Shaw trotted up the ramp, and inside he zig-zagged past six machine gun mounted jeeps. Looking forward, he saw some soldiers sitting. Then he heard a whining sound at his back, the rear door closing. He continued walking to an empty seat in the front. Once there, he placed his duffle bag under the seat, sat down, and strapped himself in. Across the aisle sat the guy who he thought talked too much. He half smiled at him.

"You finally made it," Henson declared.

Shaw grinned and said, "Not quite yet, my man. There's still 363 to do."

CHAPTER 3
Dong Ha

The huge rubber tires on the C-130's landing gear hit the asphalt airstrip at Dong Ha and screeched loudly. The plane bounced like a low thrown baseball. Inside, however, it felt like a crash landing. Every muscle in Shaw's slender body stiffened. He hadn't been so scared since the time an irate girlfriend stuck a cocked .38 caliber pistol to his head and said, "Nigga! I'll blow your brains out! Got nerve enough to say you quit me after all I've done for ya!"

Only when the plane bounced again, not as hard as before, did Shaw realize the landing was going to be safe. Still, it was the worst landing that he had ever experienced. He shook both wrists as if to restart the circulation in his arms, and he exhaled a deep breath.

The way the plane touched down was simply the appropriate introduction to Dong Ha. During the flight, he learned that the Marine base at Dong Ha was one of the U.S.'s most northern, making it close to North Vietnam. The base was located just under the demilitarized zone, the neutral buffer of land—initialed DMZ—about six miles wide, separating the two Vietnams. He had been told that in Dong Ha one could take a good set of field glasses and look across the DMZ and see the North Vietnamese maneuver their tanks.

Soon after the C-130 coasted to a stop, its cargo door eased open until it touched the airstrip.

Up front, where the passengers sat, one of the flight-helmeted airmen ordered, "Hurry and unload."

Shaw was the first to grab his duffle bag and jog out the rear of the airplane. He hadn't felt safe in the plane from the moment the pilot hit the runway.

At the bottom of the cargo ramp, Shaw slowed to a walk and looked at the sky. Gray clouds hid the sun, and because of the chilly weather, he could faintly see his breath.

A squad of jeeps with drivers sat parked right off the airstrip, parallel to the plane. Shaw could hear their engines idle as he stood waiting for the small group to unload.

"Load here!" the driver in the first jeep yelled.

Shaw, being the only one off the ramp, turned and walked toward the jeep. It had a faded green top. And like the rest of the jeeps, Army 1139th was marked in white on the front bumper.

The driver, a specialist 4th class, jumped out of the jeep. He landed off balance, and his helmet fell to the ground. He bent his long, lean frame forward, grabbed the steel pot and replaced it over his blond crop. He took three long strides and then lifted the flap in the canopy at the rear of the vehicle.

When Shaw stepped close, the specialist focused his gray eyes on him and said, "Put that duffle bag in here."

Shaw took the bag off his shoulder and sat it on the damp ground. He partially circled the bag, looking for his serial number and name. He never liked to lay his bag with the serial number and name down. They were about the only thing which differentiated one duffle bag from another. He realized only one bag would be in the jeep, but it had become a habit for him to make sure the black stenciled letters and numbers on the green, Army bag were up.

"God dammit, hurry up, so we can get off this airstrip," the driver declared, flicking ashes from his cigarette.

Shaw slung the bag into the back and stepped away.

The specialist closed the canopy, but he had trouble zipping it shut. "God dammit, this sticks all the time," he exclaimed as his long, bony fingers fought with the zipper.

Shaw looked at the specialist's trembling hands and figured they were the trouble. "Let me try."

"Go 'head," the specialist snapped.

Shaw stepped toward the canopy and grabbed it with his left hand. With his right hand he pulled the zipper until it completely closed the flap. Then he went and sat down in the passenger seat without saying anything or looking at the specialist; he figured the specialist felt insulted, and he knew from the streets of Naptown that it would be best not to say anything.

Over his jungle shirt the specialist wore a flak jacket— a green, nylon, sleeveless jacket that was padded with a tough fiber material which impeded shrapnel.

The specialist had actually outstepped Shaw to the front seats. Now he clutched, then rammed the floor mounted stick into first gear. When he accelerated, red mud kicked from the rear tires, and Shaw's head jerked backward. Then the specialist quickly shifted to second gear.

Why was he so nervous, Shaw wondered.

The driver went to third gear, jerking Shaw's head again.

Shaw's patience expired. "Why in the fuck don't you slow down, man, before you get us both killed!"

"If I don't hurry and get away from this airstrip, we will get killed!"

Shaw's heart pounded like a sledge hammer. "What the fuck do you mean?"

The driver's bright, gray eyes were fixed on the bending road when he answered. "Nearly every time a plane lands, Charlie starts shooting them damn rockets in. A couple of days ago they got a direct hit."

"On a jeep?" Shaw inquired, his voice pitched at alto, an octave higher than normal.

"Naw. A C-130."

The pitch of Shaw's voice relaxed to tenor. "As big as they are, how they gonna miss?"

"They do. And most of the time. The planes land in different places. And Charlie always has to move his launching pads 'cause we return heavier fire once our radar gives us the projectory of the rockets. It's a rough location. The problem is that them damn rockets come from a lot of different places." His eyes shifted to the corner. "Look to the right. That crater was made by one of those rockets."

"I saw some earlier. I thought they were shallow foxholes."

Abruptly, the specialist, Lee marked on the right side of his helmet cover, grinned. He even slowed down. "Foxholes! You real green."

Shaw frowned and said, "Hey, Lee, when do I get my gear?"

"I'm taking you to batallion headquarters now. They'll issue you that shit, and you'll get some more when you get to your battery."

Shaw's lips curled upward. "You mean I might not get assigned to Dong Ha after all!"

Lee laughed. "Maybe not. Maybe Khe Sanh."

Shaw caught the sarcasm in his laugh. "Khe Sanh must be worse?"

"Khe Sanh *was* suicide! Every day for a month Charlie hit them sorry ass Marines with every kind of rocket and artillery they had. The 1st Air Cav started a push the other day. They're going in and kick Charlie's ass, so the Marines can get the hell out. It's not too bad now."

Shaw had heard the story: the Cav was the first unit in Vietnam to effectively utilize the mobility of the helicopter; that mobility was what Charlie feared most.

"Why you call the Marines 'sorry'? They're supposed to be tough."

"Shit. Okay, they are. They're just outdated. Most of them are still fighting with M-14s and World War II 60mm mortars. In the Nam, the M-16's the rifle."

With one hand Lee effortlessly lifted the black rifle by its sight. The sight was center mounted and made like a carrying handle. The butt of the rifle was made of hard plastic. The weapon weighed six pounds, two-and-a-half pounds less than the M-14.

Lee handed the rifle to Shaw. When Shaw grasped it, Lee released his hold and said, "If you was trained like I was, I know you've never handled a M-16."

"Yeah, you're right. Just a M-14."

Shaw balanced the rifle with one hand and looked it over, muzzle to stock like a child eyeing a new toy.

"It's a good rifle," Lee commented. "A lot of guys complain 'cause they jam. And they will if . . ."

" 'They're not kept clean,' " Shaw inserted instantly.

"How did you know that? Well, anyway, if you can

get a new one with the chrome bolt, you won't have any problems. Just keep it halfway clean."

"A chrome bolt, huh."

"When we stop, I'll show you what it looks like."

Shaw grinned. "So you got one?"

"Yep."

They headed away from the airstrip along a dirt road at 30mph. The surrounding terrain was flat and bare. Hovels sat scattered off the road. The shabby dwellings were makeshifts of reused plywood and flattened cans with roofs of bambo and thatch.

The road quickly led them to the entrance of another compound where a military policeman waved the jeep through the gate.

Inside the compound, green tanks marked U.S. Marines maneuvered. Marines, whose uniforms only differed from soldiers by the absence of unit patches and namestrips, were filling sandbags or unloading supply trucks from almost any point along the main road.

After driving several hundred feet and past dozens of brown barracks, Lee turned onto a side road and drove slowly past a few barracks before braking. "This is it, buddy."

The barrack looked like all the others, except the gray sign which read 1139th Artillery Battalion Headquarters. The words were in red while the emblem of two crossed cannon barrels was in black. The two foot by two foot sign was nailed secure just above the door.

Lee moved the gearshift to neutral, then pulled the handbrake. He went to the canopy and unzipped the flap.

Shaw followed and retrieved his duffle bag.

"That's it for me," said Lee, looking at the dark

lenses of Shaw's glasses. "My job was to get you here."

Shaw automatically reached out for a handshake, but then he noticed a bewildering stare on Lee's face. Just as he was ready to withdraw his hand, Lee slowly extended his long arm. His hand was open.

"Thanks for getting me here all right," Shaw said, shaking Lee's hand in the traditional manner. "How much time have you got left here?"

A smile widened his face. "Twenty-one days."

"No wonder you couldn't work that zipper when we were at the airstrip." Shaw then slung the duffle bag over his shoulder and started walking toward headquarters barrack. Several seconds later he heard the seat squeak behind him and then the idle of the engine increase.

Beep, the horn sounded, catching Shaw by surprise. He turned.

Lee was waving briskly. "So long now," he said while easing off.

Shaw returned the wave. A smile lit his face. He suddenly felt very welcome to the country. He knew that the collective warmth of Specialist Lee and brother Myers was the reason. He also sensed that the troops formed a tighter relationship in the Nam than in the States. *Maybe they believe in Lieutenant Sargent's philosophy: 'Our success will depend on how well we work together.'*

He spun and started walking back towards headquarters.

Four soldiers, three white and one black, filled and stacked sandbags in front of the barrack. They stopped when Shaw approached.

"What it be like with the sisters back home?" the

tall, dark brown skinned soldier asked. His face was clean shaven, unblemished, and handsome. He favored a youthful Sidney Poitier.

Shaw stopped. His shaded eyes caught the top of the soldier's fatigue cap and quickly moved down 72 inches to the toes of his dusty boots. Then Shaw looked him in the eye and answered, "They still there, looking good and wearing them big, pretty afros!"

"I'll be right there with them in two more months, homey," the soldier said with a smirk. His namestrip read Johnson. He wore the PFC rank insignia on the upper sleeves of his jungle utilities.

Shaw was a little discouraged that Johnson was still only a PFC after spending ten months in Vietnam. He had always been told that it was easy to make rank in the Nam because of the high degree of turnovers due to completed tours and casualties.

"This is headquarters, isn't it?" Shaw asked, pointing at the door, knowing it was.

"Yeah, homey," Johnson said. "This is it! The 1139th Home of the sandbag fillers!"

The white soldiers, all PFCs, laughed.

It dawned on Shaw that Johnson's outspokenness was the reason he was still a PFC. The plywood shutters across the screen windows of the headquarters barrack were lifted halfway; Shaw figured that Johnson was indirectly telling his superiors about his displeasure with being on the sandbag detail.

The tone of Johnson's voice matured. "Go on in," he said. "You'll see Sergeant Robinson in the first office on the left."

"Okay. Thanks," Shaw spoke, setting his duffle bag down. He planted one foot on the first door step, took two more steps and was at the door. He pushed it open. It led to a flourescent hallway. On each side there were three offices, a title plate above the door of each. The plate over the first office on the left read NCO in Charge. Shaw quietly stepped to the door. He could hear music and someone typing. He knocked.

"Come in," someone quickly responded.

Shaw opened the door and walked into the office. The neat arrangement of a metal shelf, file cabinet, two chairs and an oak desk took up most of the space in the room. The fancy, gold lettering of the name plate on the desk spelled out Sgt. First Class Olson Robinson.

"Close the door. I like privacy."

Besides Robinson's bass pitched voice, the next thing that struck Shaw was the length of his afro. It was two or three times longer than his own. He judged that Robinson was in his forties, and assumed that he was a career soldier, though all career non-commissioned officers that he had encountered before wore a more conservative hair style, close cut on the sides. Shaw was sure that Robinson realized the Army considered the longer afros objectionable. So what he had been told in Ft. Lewis, he thought, must really be true: duty in Vietnam was less stringent when it came to dress, hair length, facial hair, and even discipline.

"Have a seat Shaw," the NCO said, sitting behind the desk, reading the field jacket name strip. Sergeant Robinson's shiny, black mustache was full yet trimmed so that it didn't fall over the ridge of his lip or curl around the corners. The glossy, black hair on his head was lightly spiced with gray on the top. His skin was oily and smooth, except for his thick wrinkled forehead, and though it was brown, it was a shade darker than Shaw's. "I got word some replacements would be coming in today. You're the first. Where did you leave from?"

"Cam Ranh Bay, sergeant."

SFC Robinson reached and turned the volume down on his desk radio. "I'm surprised no other replacements accompanied you. Evidently, they're coming in from Tan Son Nhut. That's much farther."

"Some other guys were on the plane. They should be on the way. I just got here fast."

As sudden as a change in the wind, Shaw said, "I didn't know we could get a radio station here?" His ears were attuned to the soul singing of Aretha Franklin. *She can get down.* He snapped his fingers gently.

"I can tell this is your first time out of the country. Anywhere we serve in numbers, there's an armed forces network station. I bet you don't know about the *Stars and Stripes,* either?"

"The *Stars and Stripes?*"

"It's a damn shame they don't teach you recruits about anything but how to fight. You know anything about this country? And don't tell me it's at war."

He ought to know I was briefed some on Vietnam before I left the States. "I know it's close to 400 miles long," Shaw added.

"You're wrong. That's just about the distance from here to Saigon, the capital."

Okay, so I had it mixed-up.

"It's closer to 600 miles long," Robinson stated. "And maybe 100 miles wide at the broadest point." He leaned forward, his dark brown popeyes fixed on Shaw's sunglasses. "What Vietnamese holiday just passed?"

Shaw sat speechless for a moment.

sunglasses. "What Vietnamese holiday just passed?"

Shaw sat speechless for a moment.

The sergeant shook his head. "Tet! You got over here right after the Tet Offensive."

"Yeah!" Shaw returned, his voice bright. "I remember reading and hearing about Tet now. We were killing about 5,000 enemy a week, compared to our 500 losses. And it was their offense!"

"Well, glad you know a little even if it's only about killings. Do you know we've lost 20,000 men in this war." Then his bulging eyes turned glassy, like he had just been knocked senseless with a right cross. In a weakened voice he responded, "I lost a nephew last year." Suddenly, the veins in his neck protruded, distinct as the canals of Mars. He spoke again, but in a stronger voice. "This is a strange mothafuckin war. There's no front line like there was in Korea—or rear, either. Even at headquarters we catch fire almost everyday. You gotta be alert every goddamn minute."

Robinson paused and finally took his glazed eyes off Shaw, but only for a second. "Enough said about this crazy war. I wanted to tell you that the *Stars and Stripes* is the armed forces overseas newspaper. The military tries to make everybody feel as much at home as possible."

"I hope they do a good job."

Robinson didn't respond to that, instead, he spoke of another matter. "I got to get down to some official business now, Shaw. I've got to get you assigned." He reached out his thickset hand. "Let me have your orders."

Shaw removed the papers from his shirt pocket and unfolded them. Sitting in a metal chair at the side of

Robinson's desk, he twisted, handing over the orders.

"It won't take long," Robinson assured.

For a couple of minutes he studied the top sheet. Then he responded, still looking at the paper, "You're a 13 echo 20, huh." The Army had numbers and codes for almost everything. 13E20 meant a MOS of artillery fire direction control. "Says here your grade was 95."

"That's affirmative."

Robinson lazily raised his head. He eyed Shaw. "That's a pretty high score. Did you take a lot of science and math courses in high school?"

"Yeah, and one semester of algebra in college."

"But did you finish?"

"I couldn't afford to. Well, maybe my mother would have borrowed the money but . . . You see she wanted me to study engineering, but really I wanted to study music. I studied engineering for a semester to satisfy her. Then I told her I was going to change over to music, and she said, 'Well you'll have to work your own way through school.' You see my father's a so-called musician, and she didn't want me to follow in his footsteps. Anyway, I quit to look for a job."

"I see. Well, I'm going to assign you to G battery. It's a searchlight unit. Although I'm not supposed to tell you—it has the lowest casualty rate in the battalion."

But Shaw already knew, too, that FDC was considered one of the safest as well as prestigious jobs in artillery. "A searchlight unit?" he said, puzzled about the unexpected assignment.

Robinson eyed Shaw as if he was a hardheaded pupil. In a sharp tone he lashed, "Let me tell you something. There's very few blacks, if any, in FDC, in this battalion.

So you might as well forget about what your MOS was in the States."

"Could I get an explanation, sergeant?"

"You sure can. And I'm going to give you a good one." He paused as he laid the papers down on the desk. "A Negro major has said he only wants men with college backgrounds of at least two years to be in FDC. He claims they function better under pressure. Now you and I both know there ain't too many blacks going to come through with two years college. Right?"

"Yeah," Shaw conceded.

"This whole thing all happened when fire direction control got sloppy and fed the wrong information to the gunners. A round fell short and killed twenty of our men."

At first Shaw looked like someone who had just been told a relative died, but within a second he blurted, "Yeah, but I know 13 echo 20 inside out. You seen my grade. I want to prevent something like that from happening again."

"I know you're sincere, but the major said a high grade and two years of college. And besides, I've already made my decision; you've got your orders—G battery. You fly to Phu Bai tomorrow. Understand?"

"Yeah, sergeant," Shaw snapped, a sneer on his face. But deep inside he wasn't as upset with the sergeant as he made it appear. Actually, he admired the way that the sergeant carried himself, his frankness.

"I'll have your orders cut this afternoon. Any other question?"

"Yeah. Where's the mess hall?"

Robinson leaned back in the wooden chair and laughed. "Shaw, get out of my office, before I go crazy trying to figure you out." The laugh dwindled. "When you go outside, turn left and go down to where the road bends. You'll see it. Come back after lunch. I'll have your orders and get you assigned to transit. Bring your duffle bag on inside."

After lunch Shaw returned to headquarters, got his orders, and received a temporary barrack assignment. He was further instructed to be on his way to Phu Bai by 0900 the next morning.

It took Shaw two-and-a-half minutes to reach the barrack tagged Transit B. He stepped inside, with the duffle bag on his shoulder, scanning the incandescent lit room for a bare bunk. Of the twelve bunks, several were without a pillow and blanket.

Three other soldiers, with private stripes, sat on the bunks in the rectangular shaped room.

"Where's supply?" Shaw asked the closest soldier.

He looked directly at Shaw, pointed to the right and said, "Two barracks down, blood."

"Thanks, man." Shaw walked over to the empty bunk and dumped his duffle bag on the mattress. The bag sank rather than bounced, as if dead weight hitting soft ground. Then he turned around and walked out.

Minutes later he returned with a pillow, white pillowcase, two white sheets, and a green blanket. He stepped to the bunk and removed the duffle bag. Then he began making the bed.

When he finished with the bunk, he decided the next order of business was a nice, hot shower. As he had left supply, he had seen the toilet and shower sheds, each half the size of the other brownish buildings. The two stood isolated at the end of headquarters compound.

While still standing by the bunk, he unlocked his duffle bag, taking out a white towel, a bar of soap, a tube of toothpaste, and a washcloth. He wrapped the paraphernalia in the towel, tucked it under his arm, snapped shut the lock and split for the shower.

He undressed inside the shower shed, then curled his arms around his bare body to buffer the chilly air as he dashed into the shower stall. Then he reached for the faucet knobs. But there was only one. He turned it until water streamed steadily. Dissatisfied with the moderate flow, he twisted the knob all the way to the left, but the flow never increased. *The hell with it.* Then, with his finger, he touched the water. It was like the air. *Maybe it has to run a little longer to warm-up.* He let it run for two more minutes, occasionally using the big toe on his right foot as a thermometer. The temperature remained constant. *I know these guys ain't taking cold showers, or are they?*

Shaw's head moved upward as his eyes followed the water pipe for the stall. The pipe came in from the single-slanted roof. With his eyes on the pipe, he backed out of the stall and then out of the shed, until he again saw the 400 gallon water tank that was secured on a platform. He stepped back inside the shed, went to the stall and turned the water off.

Shaw dressed, and left the shower shed, shaking his head. As far as he was concerned, it was at least a warm shower or stay funky. And he doubted that he would get that shower in Dong Ha.

He walked by the toilet shed as he headed back to the barrack. The odor surrounding the shed was so strong that he placed his hand over his nose. The toilets had no plumbing at all. They were like the tall, portable latrine he had once used on bivouac: the waste was collected in an open, cut down, metal drum, placed directly under and two feet away from the stool. Standard operating procedure was to remove the drum and burn the waste with kerosene at the end of the day. However, the odor lingered out as the day warmed and wore.

"Ah," someone in the toilet shed sighed.

Shaw stopped. He decided to ask whoever was in the head about the showers. He eased his hand away from his nose; he didn't want to offend whoever was sitting on the stool.

Shaw stepped to the shed and pulled open the screen door. He saw just one soldier as he walked inside. The thick-framed, young, white soldier sat on one of the four stools. Shaw inquired, "How come all the water is cold in the showers?"

The curly, red-headed soldier looked up for a second time. With his bright, brown eyes he stared at Shaw for a moment. "Ha, ha," he suddenly laughed. "Hey, boy, we not gonna waste no kerosene by keeping those burners on the tank going all day. We don't fire up the burners 'til after dinner, ya hear."

The soldier's southern accent and tone of voice reminded Shaw of a white dude that he had chewed out in basic, who had gotten his attention by saying, "Hey, nigger."

Shaw retaliated. He gave the red-head the menacing stare Joe Louis gave Max Schmelling just before he knocked him out. Then with his thumb and forefinger, Shaw squeezed his own nostrils.

The soldier got the message. His face went red with anger.

Shaw turned, pushed the door and walked out of the shed.

The next morning at 0900, the air cool like the day before and the sky partly sunny, Shaw left headquarters compound by jeep. He headed for the airstrip to board a helicopter that would depart for Phu Bai at 0950.

"Where is Phu Bai?" Shaw questioned the driver, the expression on Shaw's face so intense that he appeared to frown. He figured that it couldn't be too far because the driver had told him that he would be flying to the Army base in a helicopter. Yesterday evening he had asked some of the guys in the transit barrack about the place, but none had heard of it.

"It's about 50 miles southeast, along highway one," the specialist returned, shifting his deep blue eyes from the road to Shaw, then to the road again.

"Ah yeah," Shaw said, breaking into a light smile. He was moving that much farther from the DMZ.

For the first time Shaw wore a flak jacket and helmet. And he carried a M-16. He examined the rifle as he rode. It reminded him of a toy—its lightness, solid black color, plastic stock, and fiberglass barrel cover. Then he leaned the rifle against the seat, the butt down. He then removed the magazine clip and extracted one of the cartridges; the metal magazine held twenty rounds. After placing the cartridge in his palm, he slightly raised and lowered his hand. To him, it seemed that the cartridge weighed a little more than half the weight of the 7.62mm M-14 cartridge. He looked at the point end of the M-16 cartridge and saw that the lead bullet was much smaller than that of the other weapon. It was like comparing a .22 caliber bullet with a .38. He turned the bottom of the brass cartridge up. It read Colt .223. He became concerned that it wouldn't have an effective range or sufficient penetrating power. *A measly .22 caliber bullet.*

Shaw re-inserted the cartridge in the magazine and laid it next to him on the seat. He lifted the black rifle again. He pulled the chamber lever and nodded in approval when the chrome bolt shined in his eyes.

Now five hundred yards from the airstrip, Shaw could just barely see the paved runway that cut across the flat and treeless terrain.

Four hundred yards away and still looking at the runway, Shaw suddenly leaned forward. In an instant he realized that he was right; it was an artillery explosion like he had seen at Ft. Sill. Then, looking like a grounded stormcloud expanding spontaneously to a burst, there was another.

Shaw's heart beat like a trackman just finishing the dash. He knew this was real, not a training exercise intended *not* to hurt or kill anyone!

Thump! the explosion finally sounded, and as loud as thunder overhead. The ground shook, just .5 on the Richter scale, but it shook!

The driver braked abruptly, throwing Shaw forward, but Shaw managed to throw up his arm and cushion his head from the windshield.

When the jeep stopped, the driver held his helmet to his head and leaped out of the vehicle. He hit the ground and laid flat. After a moment he raised his head, noticing Shaw still in the jeep, his head and arms against the windshield. "Jump out!"

Shaw heard him, but was too dazed from the impact to move.

The next thing Shaw knew, the driver was tugging on his arm and saying, "Get out! Get out! Are you all right?"

For a moment Shaw said nothing, then lazily looked up and answered, "Yeah, I'm all right."

The driver released Shaw's arm and dove to the ground.

Shaw dove, too, landing next to him on the hard, cool ground.

With his face pinned to the ground, Shaw counted the explosions. They came nearly every seven seconds. Although the intensity of the explosions varied, none seemed to be coming close. He had counted sixteen rounds.

As the frequency abruptly slackened to one round every forty seconds, they both stood up and looked to the airstrip in the distance. Billows of black smoke rose slowly from the wreckage of a burning aircraft on the runway.

Suddenly the thunderous sounds of firing cannons came from the direction of the 1139th. They rang out every two or three seconds.

"Give Charlie hell!" the sandy head driver yelled, poking a clenched hand in the air while stooping and retrieving his helmet from the ground with the other.

Then he turned to Shaw. "Did you get hurt when I made that quick stop?"

"Not much. You mostly scared the hell out of me when you jumped. I thought a rocket was coming in on us."

"I always hit the dirt, whether they whistle by or

not. I figure if I can hear or see the explosion, that's close enough."

The driver started toward the vehicle. "Come on get in the jeep. That's all the action we'll get today, I hope."

Shaw brushed off his clothes and stepped in the jeep.

The other soldier first removed his flak jacket and then sat in the driver's seat.

"What's your first name?" Shaw asked, his tone bright.

"Jerry. Jerry Grooves."

"I'm Jimmy. Let me shake your hand and thank you for getting me out of the jeep."

Grooves blushed. "Oh, it was nothing," he said, his hand gripped tight by Shaw's.

When Shaw and Grooves reached the airstrip, a bulldozer was pushing the burning wreckage off to the side, and a crew was filling the crater which had closed the runway. Also now, the cannons from the 1139th stopped firing.

Shaw had counted sixty-two rounds.

"That aircraft Charlie got wasn't big enough to be a C-130," Shaw said, watching the bulldozer clear the runway of the smelted craft.

"Definitely not. I think it was a Chinook."

"A Chinook helicopter! That might have been the one I was going to fly in!"

"It might have been," Grooves added, keeping his eyes on the road as he approached the small, hanger-shaped terminal straight ahead.

Grooves reached the terminal and parked his jeep in front of it. There was a squad of soldiers standing nearby, watching the repair of the runway.

"Anybody get hurt?" Grooves questioned as he stepped from the jeep.

"Naw," two soldiers answered simultaneously.

Grooves turned back toward the jeep where Shaw was removing his duffle bag. "I can see now it wasn't helicopter," said Gooves. "It was a F-4 jet. You'll be flying out in that Chinook over there." He pointed toward a long-bodied, green helicopter that had blades on both the head and tail ends.

Shaw had removed his bag and was looking fifty yards down the airstrip where Grooves pointed.

Grooves sat down in the jeep. He lit a cigarette with his lighter and took a deep breath. A moment later he exhaled. The smoke drifted skyward as he glanced at his wristwatch. "It's 9:35. Your copter should be leaving on time. It doesn't have to use the runway."

"Okay, my man."

"Maybe I'll see you in Dong Ha again," Grooves said, just as Shaw took his first step toward the helicopter.

Shaw's lean body came to a dead stop. He spun around and laughed. "I hope not, and it's not because I got anything against you."

"I know what you mean," Grooves added, nodding his head.

Then he got in the jeep, said, "Later," and took off.

Shaw watched the jeep accelerate down the dirt road for a moment, then turned and started back to the helicopter.

When he reached the Chinook, a specialist 5th class was directing soldiers into the craft. Shaw handed over his orders. The specialist simply handed them back.

"We're going to Phu Bai, little brother," the tackle-sized specialist spoke. "That where you going?"

"Yeah, man."

"Just step on board then."

As Shaw walked inside the aircraft, he could see the M-60 machine gun poking out the window on the opposite side. He gathered the helicopter was large enough to hold two squadrons of men. But, other than the pilot, co-pilot and machiner gunner, only five other soldiers sat onboard. However, three cardboard containers as large as lion cages filled up the rest of the craft.

A few minutes after Shaw buckled himself in, the specialist 5th class boarded. He pushed a button, and the door shut. Then he moved into position to man the machine gun on the near side.

Outside, the blades revolved to a beat, then gradually increased to a whip. Slowly, the aircraft fluttered into the air like a dove, rising at an angle nearly perpendicular to the ground. Then at tower top it angled off at 45 degrees, leaving the Dong Ha Marine base to disappear in the rear view.

CHAPTER 4
Phu Bai

As Shaw felt the helicopter curl and descend, his heavy eyelids rose open like a weighted balloon. He turned his head and body to the porthole behind him and saw the airstrip below. At first glance he thought that he was landing back at Dong Ha. But when he noticed there were nearly twice the number of hangers, he knew that the copter was coming into Phu Bai.

Within minutes after the Chinook landed, the specialist 5th class opened the door. "This is Phu Bai." Then he paused as he stared at a sleeping officer. "Wake up captain!" he said, enough meanness in his voice to intimidate a general.

The Army captain's grayish-blue eyes flashed open, and he straightened up in his seat.

"The flight officer leaves me in charge, sir!" the specialist spoke as meanly as before. Then he glanced at the other soldiers with his deep brown eyes. "I want everybody to grab their shit and be off my plane in the next minute. I'm already running five minutes late."

Forty seconds later the six men had deboarded the aircraft. Shaw was the last to leave. He now stood behind the other men as he looked left then right, wondering why there wasn't a bus or jeep near the landing pad.

The specialist stood in the copter doorway, shaking his head. Then he cupped his large, dark hands around his mouth and yelled above the noise of the craft's engine. "You cats can call your units from the terminal. They'll send somebody over in a ride and pick you up, or you can stand here all day like a bunch of dummies."

The small terminal was practically devoid of passengers as Shaw spoke on the wall phone. "Connect me with G battery, 1139th Artillery," he instructed the operator while he cupped his hands around the phone receiver and pressed it hard to his ear; the sound of a jet taking off nearly drowned out everything.

After several seconds someone spoke. "This is Master Sergeant Crump, 1139th Artillery."

"Yeah, sergeant, I just flew in from the 1139th in Dong Ha. I got orders for G battery here."

"Give me your name and rank, soldier. I'll have someone there in ten minutes. Wait inside the terminal. He'll have you paged on the intercom." Shaw gave the sergeant his name and rank, hung up the phone and waited. Fifteen minutes later his name was announced over the PA. He was told that a jeep was waiting for him in front of the building.

Shaw rose lazily from the duffle bag that he had been sitting on next to the wall. He slung it over his shoulder and grabbed the rifle by its scope mount, which looked and served as a luggage handle. Then he walked out of the terminal and stopped right outside the metal doors. There were at least ten other soldiers standing outside. Only when one of them moved forward, could Shaw see a jeep five meters down which had G/1139th painted in white on the green, front bumper. Almost as soon as he made his first step toward the jeep, it pulled to the front of the terminal to a spot a truck had just vacated. So, when the jeep came to a halt, Shaw was standing next to it.

"I'm PFC Shaw," he said, trying to get the attention of the driver, who wore no helmet and was looking past him.

The driver jerked his kinky head toward the voice of Shaw. "Aw. You got on private stripes. I was looking for PFC stripes."

"My fault. I haven't had a chance to get my new stripes."

"No problem. I should have figured that. Anyway, you can buy some at the PX and have them sewn on by one of the Vietnamese girls working around camp. It'll cost, but not much. Everything's cheap here, man. Grass is a dollar a joint, and you can get a shot for five dollars."

Oh boy, Shaw wondered. He had shot some boy when he was sixteen, trying to be hip. He remembered the high as nice and mellow right before he passed out. He spent a day in the hospital because he had shot too much of the heroin for his virgin system. After he recovered, he vowed to himself and his mother never to touch any such drug again. "A shot of what?" he checked.

The driver giggled. "You know. Some trim."

"Aw, that," Shaw said with a smile. "The first time I bought some I was in Lawton, Oklahoma, stationed at Fort Sill. I was in a club when a sister hit on me for a date. She was cute and had a pretty smile, man. I was kind of naive then; I thought she really wanted me to take her out and show her a good time. She told me to walk her back to her apartment so she could change clothes. When we got there, she changed clothes all right. She got butt naked and said, 'It's going to cost you fifteen dollars.' I started to tell her buying sex ain't my thing, but her slim, yellow body was nice."

"Was she hairy?" the three striped sergeant asked, probably wanting to year yes. It would have been a desirable change since the average Vietnamese woman had a scant amount of pubic hair. The sergeant's eyes were wide open as if the woman Shaw had spoken of was right in front of him.

Shaw instantly answered. "Halfway from her navel down, a thick, black forest, man!" He paused like he would in an up-tempo piece that had a full note rest. "So I took the last twenty out of my pocket and said give me my change and let's get it on."

"Haa . . .," the sarge laughed, his head back and his mouth open so wide that Shaw could see the silver fillings on his molars. Then he stuck out the palm of his hand. "Give me some play."

Shaw reached out his hand and slapped it palm down on the sergeant's, then they broke into a frenzy of laughter.

When the laughter dwindled, the sergeant spoke. "Throw your gear in the back so we can get back to base camp before that fool, Sergeant Crump, lists me AWOL."

Shaw stood outside of the orderly room. He knew the first order of business was to report to the commanding officer, Captain Delaney. He removed his flak jacket, pulled his jungle shirt straight and adjusted the helmet on his head until it felt level. He wanted to take advantage of the fact rank came fast here. Impressing the commanding officer was a good start, he thought. The higher the rank he could make, the more money he could send home to have put in the bank and to help his mother.

Shaw stacked his gear outside, then stepped into the orderly room. The first man to greet him sat at a desk. The nameplate read Master Sergeant W. J. Crump.

"You must be Private First Class Shaw," the balding sergeant said in a gravel voice. Military horn-rimmed glasses sat low on his long, pointed nose.

"Affirmative, sergeant," Shaw returned crisply, standing stiff at attention.

"The CO's waiting to see you. He's in the last office straight back."

Shaw pivoted 90 degrees and stepped down the hall. He passed two other offices before he stopped at the doorway of Captain Delaney's office.

"Come in, come in," the Captain said, standing behind a polished walnut desk. He emitted an image of youthfulness: a full head of curly, brown hair and a smooth, bare face. As he looked Shaw in the eye, his head tilted upward a notch.

Shaw walked in the office, stopped in front of the desk, then saluted.

The captain returned the salute and quickly brought his hand down. "Our unit is a special detachment to the 1139th. We're unique in a sense. Everyone that first comes into the unit wants to know what the hell a searchlight does in Vietnam besides get shot at. Well, it guides in aircraft at night on the LZs and airfields. It provides illumination for perimeter guard. And, it searches for the enemy at night using infra-red light. So you see this light might be anywhere doing any number of jobs. Do you think you're ready for it?"

"Yes sir!" Shaw said loud and clear.

A broad smile appeared on the captain's face. "Well, you've been picked to go to the 3rd platoon, which works exclusively with the Marines. The 3rd is based in Da Nang. Lieutenant Green is the executive officer, and Sergeant Underwood is the platoon sergeant."

The captain took his eyes off Shaw and read the note on his desk. Then he lifted his head, stroked back the locks of brown hair with his fingers and said, "Coincidentally, Sergeant Underwood is coming in from the field today for re-supply. I'm sure he'll leave in the morning with the convoy. You can leave with him. So go to supply and get your footlocker. The sergeant in supply will show you where the transit barrack is."

"Yes sir."

Smiling, the captain reached out an open hand.

Shaw followed, and they shook hands.

"Welcome to G battery," the captain finally greeted. "Do your best to keep it a proud unit."

"Yes sir!"

While Shaw stood at the front counter of the supply room, the supply sergeant grumbled from the rear of one of the shelved storage aisles. "Looks like we're out of size 8½ jungle boots. How about 9s?"

"That's all right. The ones I got on should last 'til you get some more."

"Okay," the regular sergeant said, his voice closer.

In a moment he was at the counter dumping an armload of clothing—solid green undershirts, shorts, socks and jungle utilities. There were five of each item, plus two sets of camouflaged utilities.

Shaw remembered from basic the drill sergeants boasting that the U.S. Army dressed and equipped its soldiers better than any other army in the world. He could see now that they were right.

Shaw took some of the items from the counter and began laying them in his foot locker next to the green towels and washcloths that he had placed there minutes earlier.

By the time Shaw removed everything from the counter, the sergeant returned with a backpack, entrenching tool, canteen, mess kit, bandolier of M-16 magazines and several boxes of ammunition. "You're ready to fight a war now," the sarge said as he laid the gear on the counter. "Three hundred rounds should get you started."

The next morning, after breakfast, Shaw loaded his duffle bag and footlocker on the bed of the three-quarter ton truck that Platoon Sergeant Underwood had pulled up in front of the transit barrack. Bench seats stretched down both sides of the high canopy covered bed.

Since Sergeant Underwood sat in the cab with another soldier, Shaw lifted himself and his rifle into the back of the truck. "Okay, I'm loaded," he yelled, wearing helmet and flak jacket like the other two.

"Smitty," the sergeant said to the specialist 4th class in the cab with him, "how about letting Shaw sit up front so I can explain some things to him?"

"Whatever you say, sarge," Smith said, insincere in

tone, as he grabbed his rifle, got out of the cab and jumped into the rear of the truck.

"What's going on?" Shaw asked; his manner was cool.

"Grab the seat up front. Sarge wants to meet you."

Shaw nodded. "Yeah?" He grabbed his weapon, then jumped out the back of the truck. In a moment he occupied the seat Smith had vacated.

The sergeant put the truck in forward gear and pulled off. Once he hit the main road, he sped by a different barrack every second and past a different unit every quarter minute or so. The road alternated between curves and straightaways, never the same for more than half a mile. "I'm trying to beat the convoy to Route 1," the mustached sergeant said. The color of his dark brown pencil-thin mustache matched the straight, short hair on the side of his head. The sergeant's bloodshot eyes cornered on Shaw. "What's your first name?"

Shaw caught a whiff of the sergeant's breath. *Last night's scotch.* He leaned toward his half open window. His movement was discreet, and the sergeant paid no attention. Shaw was unmistaken about the smell of scotch on anyone's breath because it was his old man's drink. Every Saturday and Sunday morning at home he smelled it in any room where his old man breathed.

"Jimmy," Shaw finally answered.

"How's about me calling you Jim?"

"Well, you can," Shaw returned, sounding reluctant, "but Jimmy sounds better to me."

A grin revealed Sergeant Underwood's tobacco stained teeth. "Okay, Jimmy. And I hope you don't think I'm crazy for driving so fast." The road was dirt. The speedometer needle pointed to 45. "But if we get caught in that convoy, we'll be almost half a day getting to

Firebase Mary Ann. Otherwise, we can get there in about an hour."

"Isn't it safer to go with the convoy?"

"It depends." He paused. "Charlie's not going to waste any time on one or two trucks. What we got to watch out for are road mines. But even that's no big problem because the engineers and Seabees go out with mine detectors to clear the roads in the mornings. Of course, I've heard incidents where Charlie will go behind the engineers and plant mines, but that was during Tet. Now, a month ago, during Tet, I wouldn't have gone a half mile without a convoy, unless it was in a tank or APC. Tet was a bitch!" he said, shaking his head. "After that, I made up my mind not to extend here for 30 days, for an early out. I'll just play it safe and do my last five months in the States. I'll have twenty years this November."

"You leave next month?" Shaw asked in a bright tone.

"Oh yeah. May 2nd. Then 30 days leave with mama, the first 10 in Hawaii. I'll see the kids after that. They're grown now."

"What was Tet like?"

"What state you from?"

"Indiana."

Sergeant Underwood smiled for an instant. "I'm from Illinois. You know how it is in the winter when 12 inches of snow falls on the ground: everybody's afraid to go out. Well, during Tet, Charlie's rockets and ground attacks fell on us like heavy snow. Until we stopped half stepping and starting kicking ass. You know, it's funny—Charlie really had us fucked up at first. We thought the little sons-of-bitches only knew how to fight guerrilla warfare."

The sergeant reached in his upper shirt pocket and pulled out a pack of Camels. He hit the bottom of the pack against the dashboard, then extended the pack toward Shaw. "Have a smoke?"

"I don't smoke."

"You look too clean-cut; I should have known. That's good, though. Hope you don't mind my smoking?"

Shaw started to say the smoke bothered him, but the sergeant had already pushed in the lighter and pulled a cigarette from the pack with his lips. Shaw made no reply as he rolled down the window a little further.

A moment later, the sergeant braked the vehicle to a stop at the camp gate.

"How far you guys going?" a soldier, with a black armband which had MP imprinted in white, asked.

"Firebase Mary Ann," Sergeant Underwood stated. It was 35 miles south on Route 1.

"There was some action on bridge Lima 9 last night. Maybe you ought to wait on the convoy that's leaving here going to Da Nang."

"How many vehicles?"

The MP looked to the side of the road where the convoy—a pair of deuce-and-a-half trucks, each mounted with a turret that had quad .50 caliber machine guns; two tank-like vehicles with twin 40mm cannons; dozens of three-quarter ton trucks; a few other two-and-a-half ton trucks and several jeeps—sat idle as more vehicles lined up in the rear. "It's probably going to be thirty-five or forty," he said, shifting his eyes on Sergeant Underwood again.

"Forget it, corporal. We'll be all right."

Wishing that the sergeant would have taken the advice of the MP, Shaw simply turned his head and looked out his window like he hadn't heard anything. He figured that to ask the sergeant to wait would show cowardice and disobedience.

The MP stepped back and waved Underwood's three-quarter ton through the gate.

Nearly three miles away from Camp Phu Bai, the truck ascended Route 1, the two lane, dirt road that cut through the mountain range. Beautiful, Shaw accessed, knowing the city with all its tall, modern buildings couldn't touch the scenery around him. The mountains rolled with green, but pocked here and there were numerous brown areas of defoilage. In most cases, napalm bombs and agent orange chemicals had done their job by burning away areas in which the enemy would have hidden.

Then, after a ten mile stretch through the mountains, the truck descended to a level more comfortable to ground soldiers. A mile after reaching ground level, Sergeant Underwood slowed as he stared at bridge Lima 9, 100 yards away. A platoon of Marines maneuvered near the bridge. Supporting 60mm mortar rounds exploded fifty yards in front of them.

"What's going on?" Shaw asked, sitting on the edge of his seat, eyeing the activity. He tasted the action, knowing he'd like to be down there with the four squads.

"Looks like those grunts are on a search and destroy mission." Suddenly Underwood braked. "Goddamn! They kicked ass last night." The bodies of nine Viet Cong in black pajamas were stacked at the far end of the bridge.

A Marine with a M-16 and two bandoliers of ammunition crisscrossing his chest motioned the truck forward. Underwood accelerated to 15mph and moved across the bridge.

Shaw, and Underwood meticulously watched the maneuvers of the Marines, who with their weapons in ready fire position, swept slowly across the field, crouched low and a few yards from each other.

As the truck moved by the slain VC, Shaw rose to see them. When he saw a severed leg with its pink-red flesh and jagged bone lying in a rich red pool not far from the main torso, he suddenly felt faint and nauseated. He sank to the seat, placing his hand over his mouth.

Underwood stopped just past the bridge. "Sickening sight, ain't it, Jimmy?" he said, observing Shaw's reaction.

Shaw removed his hand and in a lifeless voice answered, "Yeah."

"Just remember, they're the same little bastards who would have wasted one of us if we hadn't got them."

"I wonder what hit that one?"

"Probably got it with a .50 caliber."

"In basic they said there was something in the *Geneva Convention* that forbidded the use of anti-aircraft and anti-armor weapons against people?"

"That's right and that's bullshit! Who in the fuck's going to be concerned with how decent he kills somebody trying to kill him!"

Shaw agreed, though not out loud. He had always thought that parts of the *Geneva Convention* were impractical, if not foolish.

As the conversation perked up, more life came into Shaw's voice. "It don't look like we lost any men?"

"If nine VC got it, we lost two or three, believe that! And probably three or four wounded. More of our men would die if it wasn't for the quick helicopter evacuation to field hospitals."

Crack! a shot rang out from a M-16.

Shaw quickly turned toward the shot, seeing the puff of white smoke. He had no fear, however, because he knew the contingent of Marines would take care of matters.

Crack, crack, shots from a different angle burst forth.

"We got a kill!" a Marine exclaimed from the field. "Cocksucker was hiding in the ditch."

"This area is hot!" Underwood exclaimed as he came off the clutch like he was in a drag race.

Scared-ass old man.

The truck sped past the water soaked rice paddies and tacky huts, occupying both sides of the road. In the background were low hills.

Shaw looked toward the rice paddies where he saw a large, brownish animal that resembled an ox. He knew it was the water buffalo. He had learned about it in a Vietnam briefing at Fort Sill. The animal served in the same general capacity as a farm horse, but not every farmer could afford to own one. Additionally, the animal was seldom butchered for meat, hide or horn because it was considered sacred by the Vietnamese people.

The truck continued speeding and stirring up dust along Route 1 until it slowed a couple of miles from Firebase Mary Ann where Sergeant Underwood downshifted to second gear. Here, he crept behind a civilian convoy—two overloaded buses that looked old enough to be made in the early '50s; a packed sub-compact car, its fenders crumbling with rust; three motorbikes and a compact truck that clattered and smoked. A U.S. military convoy was passing in the opposite direction.

When the convoy in front of Underwood's truck stopped, he had to follow suit.

Underwood and Shaw both looked on as two Vietnamese women got off one of the buses and jogged to the side of the road by some brush. Each woman was dressed in a pair of black satin pants, a pale blouse and a wide, light colored, brimless straw hat that was cone shaped and low cut. At the brush the two women pulled down their pants and squatted. Shaw stared hard at the side of the road where he could plainly see them behind the budding brush. He didn't want to believe what he saw.

Then, as if reading Shaw's mind, the sergeant spoke. "Yeah, they're taking a shit. Just think, we're over here fighting and getting killed for these primitive people. They don't even carry toilet paper."

On the other side of the road a quad fifty, like the caboose of a train, signaled the end.

The sergeant accelerated and drove around the tail of the civilian convoy, commenting, "I got to get around this heap of junk." He stayed in the left lane until he passed the carcass of a water buffalo, the reason the convoy had stopped.

"Did you see that, sarge? That water buffalo's entire guts blown out!"

"I saw it," Underwood stated, a lack of concern in his voice. "That's about two hundred-fifty dollars US money, just blown away. That's a lot of money to these people. I hear they'd rather lose a baby than a water buffalo; they know they can make a baby anytime."

Shaw's voice hardened with contempt: "You don't like Vietnamese, do you?"

The sergeant took his eyes off the road and looked curiously at Shaw, probably to see whether the expression on his face showed the same seriousness as his voice.

Shaw's face yielded no signs of playfulness.

"They're all right," the sergeant returned gingerly. It's just that I've seen too many guys flown away in plastic bags. And the officers tell me those guys gave up their lives for a good cause, to keep these poor people from being overrun by communists." He shook his head in disgust. "Big deal. These fuckin people don't even seem to care."

Shaw wanted to tell Sergeant Underwood that he didn't dig the war either and that he sure didn't want to be over here, but why take it out on the Vietnamese. But, he thought it best that he didn't tell him. Instead, he said, "I can understand how you feel."

"Well," the sergeant said, letting out a deep breath, "we'll be at the firebase in a few minutes. You'll be working with Sergeant Kennedy and Spec. 4 Carpenter. When you get broke in, Carpenter will be going to Da Nang. He's a short timer."

"How many days has he got left?"

"Don't get envious, but he's got about forty-five left. I try to get all my men out of the field when they get that short."

"That's all right," Shaw said, his cheeks raised and lips curled. "Let me see." He thought for a couple of seconds. "That means I only got 315 days to really worry about."

"You worry about every day here!" the sergeant

barked. "I seen a Marine corporal get hit with a RPG in Da Nang, and he only had seven days left."

"Did he die?"

"He got hit in the chest with a weapon designed for tanks," the sergeant answered, seemingly unmoved. But then, he dropped his head. A moment passed before he raised it and returned his eyes to the road.

"Aw," Shaw said, the pitch of his voice flat, the expression on his face like when he embarassed himself on leave as he asked about a friend who, he was finally told, had been dead for months, accidentally shot in the temple at a party.

CHAPTER 5
Firebase Mary Ann

There were five, ground-level guard posts sitting 70° apart inside the perimeter surrounding the firebase. The base was the size of a major league baseball park. Three rows of concertina barbed wire stacked like a pyramid, encircled it. Solid colored sandbags, blue grass green and earth brown, fortified the guard posts and the nearly three dozen bunkers scattered inside the base. A couple of large tents stood staked next to the shade of a grove of young trees. The trees were the only ones within the perimeter.

Where the road didn't run tangent to Mary Ann, open rice fields and a grove of rubber trees surrounded the base. On the other side of the road, for hundreds of yards, was open field infested with weeds and wild shrubs. For the next few miles rose rows of hills, brown in some areas, green in others. The background for the hills was an extended mountain range, piercing the clouds at numerous points.

As Sergeant Underwood drove through the shrubless compound, Shaw saw the battery of 155mm howitzers, each semi-circled by a shallow wall of sandbags. He smelled the burnt gunpowder—a clue that the cannons had been fired recently. The six cannons pointed toward the hills. Shaw noted the elevation on the guns. At 45° he knew they were set for maximum distance. He figured the crew was using a moderate charge, four powder bags to hurl the 95 pound explosive.

That meant the target was at the base of the mountains, almost seven miles away.

The sergeant parked the vehicle near a bunker at the far side of the compound. "Get your gear, Jimmy. This is home for awhile."

Shaw got out of the truck and stretched. He had been in the truck an hour and twenty minutes. Then he went to the back of the truck where Smitty was pulling the foot locker and duffle bag forward, "Thanks," said Shaw. "I can get 'em from here."

"All right," Smithy said, stepping aside.

Shaw grabbed the foot locker by the handles at the long ends of the rectangular box. He turned and looked at the square-like bunker. It was a few steps higher than basement level and enveloped with sandbags. The Seabees had built the sturdy bunker with wooden struts and poured concrete.

Shaw, with the thirty pound foot locker, stepped down into the bunker. It was lit partly by the sunlight coming thru the narrow passageway. The other light source was a 100 watt bulb, hanging from the plywood ceiling, seven feet from the dirt floor. The electricity for the bulb and a portable refrigerator was supplied by the camp's main gasoline generator.

Three unfolded cots sat along each plywood wall. On two of them laid a poncho liner, so Shaw lowered the foot locker down beside the empty cot. The ground was noticeably damp. It reminded him of the time when he walked into a damp cave and found it full of daddy longleg spiders. Feeling creepy, he shivered. Then he looked around the bunker. Once he clearly saw no spiders, he steadied himself and walked back outside to the truck.

Shaw then lifted the duffle bag from the bed of the

truck, turned and stared at the puptent next to the bunker. Two other soldiers were standing at the rear of the vehicle now. "What about the tent?" Shaw asked, looking the three-striped sergeant in the face.

"It's ours. You can stay in it if you want to." A grin was on the sergeant's hard face. His namestrip read Kennedy. "That is, if you're not afraid of incoming sniper fire and mortar rounds. It usually comes from the village down the road. Plenty of VC in it." On old, half inch scar ran horizontal over the sergeant's left eyebrow. He was in his early twenties. Built like a linebacker, he had broad shoulders and thick thighs. His flat cheeks and broad chin made his face more rectangular than oval.

"Never mind," Shaw spoke, accepting the round-about advice of Sergeant Kennedy.

Underwood eyed Kennedy and said, "Break Jimmy in quick, Bill. He's going to be Carp's replacement."

Kennedy stepped toward Shaw and reached out an open hand. "Glad to have you," he said, and they shook hands in the traditional manner.

"I'm sure glad you're here!" Spec 4 Carpenter said, his small lips curving upward. "Now I can get to base camp." Then he shifted his medium brown eyes to Underwood. "How much longer am I going to be here, sarge?" He spoke with a distinct New England accent.

"I'll be back through in three or four days."

"Good. I'll be ready."

Kennedy spoke, his bluish eyes on Shaw. "Have you zeroed your rifle?"

"Naw. I don't even know how to break it down and clean it!"

"Okay, Carp," said Kennedy, "take Jimmy to the range, then show him how to clean his rifle."

"I got you, sarge."

Shaw turned and faced the Army jeep that was parked next to the tent. His eyes became glued to the spotlight. It was 25 inches diagonal and mounted in back of the canopy covered jeep in such a way that it could be pivoted 270°. "Is this it?" He asked, the spotlight attracting him forward. He stopped at the light, reached out and touched it. "Wow, man, I bet it's powerful."

"Yeah," Kennedy commented.

"Well," Underwood spoke, a tinge of boredom in his voice, "me and Smitty better be getting back to Da Nang."

"Bring us a goddamn sundry pack and a case of Cokes next time," Kennedy demanded with a smirk.

"I'll do that. See you guys in a few days."

Underwood and Smitty proceeded to the truck, got in the cab and then drove out of the compound.

"That's some darn good shooting," Carpenter complimented Shaw. The target was a tall tree on the outside of the compound, 100 yards away. Every time Shaw had hit the narrow tree at chest height, a piece of bark had shot outward.

With his long, narrow fingers Shaw adjusted the elevation and windage notches on the bore sight. "I think I got it zeroed perfect now. Let me shoot again."

Crack, the rifle sounded, and Shaw felt little recoil as he fired it. Almost instantly he saw the bullet hit exactly where he had aimed. "The rifle feels good, man. I like it."

"Run off a clip on automatic. You will be surprised."

Shaw extracted the nearly empty magazine and inserted

a full one. He flipped the lever from semi-automatic to automatic and put the weapon at his hip.

"Now spray it!" Carpenter stated.

Cra-ac-ac-ac-ac...ack, it went, ripping off the twenty rounds in just under two seconds.

Bark shot from several trees, including the one he initially pointed the muzzle at.

"It's all right, man!" exclaimed Shaw.

"You got the swing of it?"

"Yeah! Yeah! I think so."

Sergeant Kennedy, Specialist Carpenter and PFC Shaw sat in the tent-covered mess hall. They consumed a hot meal—spaghetti and meat sauce, garlic toast, and buttered peas. Toss salad and cherry pie was on the side. They ate out of paper plates and used plastic utensils. Each drank tea or milk from their metal, canteen holder.

Speaking to Shaw the sergeant said, "Get full on this stuff. We might not get another hot meal today. It'll probably be C-rats for dinner. You tasted them?"

Shaw shook his head side to side while swallowing a bite of food.

"Only three or four meals taste like anything," added Carpenter. Seven different meals came to a case of ten. Generally each case was the same. One of the more popular meals consisted of canned beans and meatballs in tomato sauce, canned cheese, crackers, canned peaches, and canned pound cake.

"What do you do with the other meals?" inquired Shaw.

"We take the good stuff out," Carpenter returned. "Like the fruit, cheese, and cakes. The rest we give or trade to the villagers. They'll eat most of it or put it on the black market."

"What are the best meals?"

"If I tell you," the spec 4 said, "that's all you'll want. I'll let you find out. You might find something I don't like."

Shaw noticed Carpenter's brown, peach fuzz sideburns which curtailed at the center of his ears. *For a man who's spent a year in the Nam, he hasn't aged like the others. He could pass for 16 or 17.* Carpenter's face was grade school smooth and the white of his eyes as bright as a newborn's.

Carpenter raised his medium frame from the folding chair and stood straight. "I'm going back to the bunker and lie down. This nice, warm weather's made me lazy." He faced Shaw. "You better get some, too. We got to go out with the light tonight," he added, stroking down some loose strands of his straight, brown hair with the backward motion of his hand. They had been blown free by a sporadic breeze that came off the sea a half mile to the east.

"I will. First I want to get the sergeant to show me how to clean my rifle." Turning toward Kennedy, Shaw continued. "Carp forgot about it."

"Okay. And call me Bill or sarge. That 'sergeant' shit's too formal. It's for the States."

The medium length, blond hair on the top of the sergeant's head was combed to the side. On the sides it tapered to where it was close cut around the hair line, almost the way the Army liked it. The Army preferred the entire side close cut; and supposedly, it did not allow long sideburns, goatee or beard.

Kennedy and Shaw followed the other soldier back to

the bunker and got their rifles. The bunker was cooler than outside, a 5° difference. For thirty minutes the sergeant instructed his PFC on the proper care and maintenance of the M-16.

On his own Shaw broke down his weapon.

"You learn pretty quick," Kennedy said, looking at the second hand on his leather strapped wristwatch. "Two-fifty-five. With a little practice you'll be able to break it down and put it back together in that time."

"I guess I shouldn't have any problem finding time to practice." It conjured thoughts of when he would spend two and three hours practicing the piano, and his mother sweetly reminding him to put some time in on school work.

Kennedy spoke, a smile on his face as he observed his spec 4 napping on the cot. "They call us the lazy outfit—we sleep almost all day. But hell, that's the time to get some sleep at this compound. The shit hits the fan every other night." The sergeant yawned. "If you don't mind, I think I'll lay right down on this rack." The cot sank a bit. "And take a nap."

Sleep and eat in the daytime and work at night. I'm gonna have to get used to this.

Shaw wasn't sleepy. He looked out the passageway and saw three black Marines standing and talking under the trees, straight ahead. Each had a M-16 slung over his shoulder. They wore fatigue caps rather than steel pots, and not one wore a flak jacket.

Shaw stepped out of the bunker with his Army cap on. The green cap looked more like those worn by baseball players, unlike the marine cap similar to those worn by railroad engineers. He headed toward the group of

Marines. He had left his rifle behind, feeling it was secure inside the compound.

It took him little time to cover thirty-five yards.

Within fifteen feet of the Marines now, one of them saw him and coolly said, "A doggie y'all. A black one at that."

A smile brightened the gingerbread shaded face of the second Marine as he looked up. He extended his arms outward. Shaw was within ten feet. "Come on over here! Shit. I ain't talked to a brother in the Army since I left Da Nang, nine months ago!"

The warmth of the second marine touched Shaw. And instantaneously, Shaw's spotless, front teeth gleemed through a grin. He shook the Marine's hand as if they were old buddies. The thumbs were on top.

Then Shaw shook the hand of the others just as vigorously.

Staring at the name strip across the Army man's shirt, the second Marine continued, "Shaw. I think I'll call you Army. Cool?"

"Aw, yeah."

"Where you from?" the second Marine asked.

"Indianapolis."

"They call me Denvo," said the second Marine. "That's supposed to be short for Denver. Ever been there?"

"Naw," Shaw returned as he glanced at Denvo's afro. *It's as long as some of the brothers' back home.* The Marine's full, kinky, black hair bulged where the cap didn't cover it on the sides. His jet black mustache hooked around the corners of his lips. With the dark glasses, Denvo reminded Shaw of someone, but he couldn't place who.

"You cats in the Army got everything," the third Marine added slow and easy. "Names on your uniforms, SP packs up the ass, every motherfuckin thang! I should have joined the Army myself." Then the expression on his darkened face changed. His face was covered with green camouflage paint, except the pit of his eyes which revealed his yellowish skin. "I'm Bibbs. From Chi," he said, dragging the i for a full second.

"Yeah," Shaw acknowledged.

"You with that searchlight unit, ain't ya?" the bony, first Marine inquired.

"Yeah."

"Glad to see they sent a brother up," Denvo intervened. "I was beginning to think the Army was like the Marines, racist—giving all the easy jobs to the white boys."

Shaw could see himself off the reflection of Denvo's dark glasses. Shaw said nothing in return. Then it suddenly dawned on him who Denvo reminded him of: H. Rap Brown, the fiery back militant.

The first Marine spoke again. "I'm Foster."

"We call him Navybean," Bibbs added. "He's a bean and meatball freak. And ain't gained a pound."

"Augusta," Foster returned, speaking to Shaw. "That's my hometown."

"Augusta?" Shaw's tone of voice gave away that he didn't know much about the city.

"In Georgia. You know," Foster insisted.

"James Brown's town," Bibbs added.

"That's all right," Foster consoled. "I know how t'is. I didn't ever know where Indianapolis was for a long time, until the cook, they call him Naptown, told me. He went on home a couple of weeks ago."

"What's his real name? I might know him," Shaw urged.

"Shit, I don't know. All I ever heard him called was Nap and Naptown."

Shaw's eyes shifted from Foster to Denvo to Bibbs. "All you guys in artillery?"

"We don't fuck with no artillery, man," Bibbs returned resentfully. "We grunts. Ground pounders. If it wasn't for us, Charlie'd overrun this base whenever he wanted to." He paused. "Being honest, though, everythang kinda works hand in hand; when we out in the bush, we definitely need the firepower of that artillery." He pointed at the battery of 155s in the center of the compound.

Bibbs had a miniature, corporal insignia pinned to his shirt collar that was folded back. The insignia was metal, painted in black. He outranked the other two Marines by a grade. He spoke and pointed again. The direction was different. "Hey, Army, we stay in that bunker over there. Right now we got to get packed for a short patrol. Come on by sometimes."

Shaw nodded.

Pop! a flare shot up from inside the dark firebase. Five seconds later white illumination spread over half the compound and a large area outside of it.

Two Marines on night guard duty at post #4 had popped the flare. "Call the commo bunker and have Sergeant Webster send that searchlight over here," the lance corporal at post #4 ordered.

The PFC briskly cranked the portable phone box, then lifted the receiver and placed it to his ear, tilting his helmet. He spoke into the phone when Webster answered. "Sarge, this is post 4. We saw some movement. But when we shot the flare, we couldn't see anything. If a gook was out there and heard the flare go up, he had time to hide."

"I know that. Now slow down some," returned the sarge.

"Can we get that Army searchlight unit over here?"

"It just turned dark, Jones. I don't think the gooks would be making any move this early." The sergeant paused. "It's only 2050 now. I'll have them over there by 2150."

"Roger and out, sarge," Jones ended, sounding more at ease since the sergeant indicated the gooks wouldn't move so early if they moved at all. PFC Jones, a twenty-year-old black, had been in the country four weeks, but already he had been involved in three firefights. In the second one he had earned the bronze star by knocking off two snipers that had another squad pinned down.

Sargeant Kennedy stepped outside his bunker when he saw night turn to day. The bright flare was drifting down on its small parachute now. Kennedy saw no other activity. He curiously looked at his wristwatch, then went back into the bunker. A moment later the phone rang. "Hello," he said as he lifted the receiver to his ear.

"Is this Sergeant Kennedy?"

"Yeah."

"This is Sergeant Webster. They need your unit at post #4 a little earlier. Can you make it about 2150?"

"No problem. Anything wrong?"

The usual—somebody claims to have seen something. Out."

Kennedy placed down the phone receiver and looked at his men. Both were lying on their cots. "Carp and Jimmy, let's go to work!"

Shaw rose without hesitation. He was fully clothed except for his boots. He spoke. "I've been waiting to see how this light works."

"Is that why we're starting out a half an hour earlier?" Carpenter asked, lying on the cot looking at the small, ticking clock on Kennedy's foot locker.

"They called," Kennedy replied. "Somebody said they saw something. Things have been too quiet the past few days, anyway. Probably was something out there."

"Aw, Bill, you know that new platoon of Marines came in from the field yesterday. They probably still seeing NVA they killed the other day."

"Maybe so. We'll just use the extra time to train Jimmy, and we'll knock off earlier in the morning."

"That sounds good," said Carpenter.

It was exactly 2150 when Shaw lifted the canopy flap on the rear of the jeep and exposed the searchlight at guard post #4.

"Now unbuckle those straps holding the light secure," Carpenter instructed Shaw.

The jeep, parked with its rear toward the perimeter, sat virtually unprotected except for the side next to the guard bunker.

"What all did you see?" Kennedy asked the lance corporal as they stood inside the guard bunker.

"I really couldn't make it out," the dark-haired Marine answered. "Jones saw something first. When he alterted me, I just saw some movement. It could have been an animal as far as I'm concerned."

"What does Jones say it was?"

A flickering candle reflected off the Marine's bluish-green eyes as he looked the soldier in the face. "A gook in the rice paddy."

"Call him down," Sergeant Kennedy said.

The lance corporal took a couple of steps. "Jones," he hollered out of the vertical slit on the side of the bunker.

A moment later Jones stepped through the rear, the only entrance.

Looking at Jones the lance corporal spoke. "I told the Army sergeant that you thought you saw a gook."

"Yeah, I did," he said, turning his short, compact frame toward Kennedy. Jones' fair, brown skin had dark green paint smeared on his forehead and cherub cheeks. His face was free of hair. His steel pot dropped low on his head. Yet, his spotless uniform fit him well, and his utility belt neatly nugged his jungle shirt to his waist. The pant legs of his uniform were bloused flawlessly around the top of his new jungle boots, and obviously he knew enough about concealment not to have them shining. "I saw his skinny silhouette."

"How? There's no moon!" Kennedy exclaimed.

"I don't need the moon when there's the stars," Jones recited as if reading poetry.

The sergeant and lance corporal looked at each other out of the corner of their eyes, a look of uncertainty on their faces.

"I started to fire," Jones rambled, "but I wanted to check with Lance Corporal Shultz first."

"You did the right thing," Shultz affirmed in a tone that practically said *thank goodness.*

Outside, Carpenter schooled Shaw. "This light has incredible range for its size. With the appropriate beam it'll reach a distant hill. I'll start the jeep and then we'll see."

"Does the engine always have to be on?"

"On white light it should be because it drains so much power, but not necessarily on infrared light." Carpenter took a pair of binocular-like glasses out of a case and sat them down on the jeep. "You'll need these to see infrared. The objects appear green. But let's shine the white light first."

Carpenter went to the front and started the jeep. He let it idle as he reversed the direction of the driver seat. He sat in the seat and grabbed the searchlight from behind. When he flipped the switch, everything in front of the beam for the first hundred feet appeared like an overexposed snapshot.

Shaw's eyes followed the beam in awe as Carpenter slowly moved the light around a section of the perimeter. He saw nothing different than in the daytime.

The other three men hurried outside. Kennedy spoke as they stationed themselves behind a stack of sandbags by the jeep. "Point to where your man saw that movement, Shultz. I'll have mine zero in on the area."

When the lance corporal pointed, Carpenter quickly swung the bright beam in that direction. Then he flipped some lever switches on the back of the searchlight; the intensity of the beam varied as it narrowed and widened.

"Nothing's out there now," Shultz stated.

"Naw," Jones agreed.

0200. Jones and Shaw talked quietly at the jeep's rear while Kennedy and Shultz dozed in the bunker and Carpenter across the front seats.

"Did you sign up for the Army, man?"

"Be for real—with a war going on?" Then Shaw caught himself. He was talking to a man who had signed up for the Marines. "Well, I don't exactly mean it like that."

"You said it right," indicated Jones. "I wouldn't 've signed up either."

"But you signed up for the Marines?"

"Are you crazy! I got drafted. At the draft station they asked for Marine volunteers so I said to myself, why not; the Marines got the reputation, and it's still only two years of service. I figure I made a good move, brother Shaw. Look at you. You in the Nam, and I know you didn't learn as much about fighting or train as hard in basic as I did in boot camp."

"How long was boot camp?"

"Thirteen long, hard weeks at Camp Pendleton."

"Where you from, anyway?"

"Watts," Jones simply answered as if he knew Shaw was familiar with the infamous section in Los Angeles that was the scene of the first major race riot in the sixties.

Shaw spoke, sarcasm in his voice. "Burning Baby, they call it now."

"Yeah. And where you from?"

"Indiana," Shaw answered, figuring Jones wouldn't

be familiar with the city because of it being so far away and bearing no black significance except for an athlete and a musician, namely Oscar Robertson and Wes Montgomery.

"Hey," Jones spoke quietly, "why don't you check out what's on the other side of the wire again?"

"Okay," Shaw returned. "I'll use infrared this time." Twenty-five minutes ago he had used white illumination. "I don't want to start up the jeep either and wake up everybody." He smiled. Then he stationed himself next to the searchlight and flicked a switch. With one hand he slowly and steadily swung the invisible beam. In the other hand he held the special binoculars to his shaded eyes. Objects were illuminated in a pale green—the barbed wire, the trees, a figure. Immediately, movement of the searchlight ceased.

Shaw's hands began to tremble, and he almost dropped the binoculars. "H...ey, Jones," he whispered, barely able to control the phonetics of his voice.

Jones grimaced with uncertainty. "What's the matter?"

"G...G...Gooks."

The Marine snatched the binoculars and aimed them where Shaw had been looking. Two hundred seventy-five feet from the wire he saw a Vietnamese dressed in the typical VC garb and shouldering an AK-47 rifle; the Vietnamese was in a crouch. Jones shifted the binoculars to the right and saw nothing. He brought them slowly back to the left, and saw two more VC ten feet to the left of the first one; the two were digging by hand. Quickly, Jones shifted the binoculars and searchlight, scanning a larger area. He saw no other enemy.

Jones laid the binoculars in the jeep with a steady hand. In a snap he unshouldered his rifle and pushed up on the magazine, checking to see if it was secure. Then he disengaged the safety lever. He whispered, "Shaw."

Shaw stood open mouthed next to the jeep. He gathered his composure and answered. "What you gonna do?"

"This is the time to hit 'em. The element of surprise. They ever teach you that in the Army?"

"This ain't the time to talk about that."

"Okay then, if you can pop that light on, I think I can take 'em all out. Grab your rifle and get low when you do; if I miss, they'll start firing back."

"I got you," Shaw indicated timidly. "I'll count like I count off a tempo. One, two, three, four—and on the next count of one I'll switch on the white beam. You be ready to fire!"

The Marine smiled, a front tooth missing from his otherwise perfect, white set. "You a musician?"

"Yeah," Shaw returned. "You one, too?"

"Naw. I'm a boxer," the Marine said as he got as low as he could. His belly touched the soft ground. His head was up and his rifle was out front. "Now count."

"One, two, three, four," Shaw counted, the cadence even and swift. On the next count a beam of light lit up the area out front.

Crack! Crack! Crack! the shots rang out, amplified by the quietness of the early morning. Barely had a second elapsed between the first and third shots.

Shaw saw three VC slump in the wet rice paddy. Three shots, three kills, he said to himself with admiration; this little motherfucker's a born killer. I'd sure hate to get in the ring with him!

Seconds later, sheer commotion erupted around guard post #4. Carpenter leaped to his feet and grabbed his rifle. The lance corporal stormed out of the bunker, the sergeant following.

"What the hell is going on, Jones?" the lance corporal demanded.

Jones put down the green handkerchief he was wiping the barrel of his weapon with and calmly answered, "Three dead gooks, Lance Corporal Shultz."

The sides of the large, green mess tent were rolled to the top, bringing in light and ventilation. Drops of rain were steered in by the gentle afternoon breeze, but the humidity caused the 74° temperature to feel more like 84°. Shaw wiped beads of perspiration from his forehead with a napkin as he had lunch for the second time at the firebase.

Jones looked at Shaw and spoke. "I hear we came over at the right time. Our bodies can get adjusted to the heat before it really warms up."

"With this only being April," returned Shaw, "I know what July and August are gonna be like!"

"Yeah," Jones grinned.

Mess hall seating was sectioned into fifths to provide aisleways. One of the end sections, however, had a small, table sign that read: Reserved for Officers & NCOs. A captain, lieutenant and sergeant rose simultaneously from one of the tables.

As Shaw sat at his table with Jones and four other

Marines, he saw the three superiors walk forward. In a matter of seconds they stopped at his table.

"Attention," Shaw barked, scooting his chair back to stand up.

"Carry on," said the captain just as the other men started to rise. The men sat back down.

"Stand up PFC Jones," the platoon sergeant said.

Jones' light colored eyes opened widely. "Me?" he asked while rising.

The captain returned. "I heard about your heroics last night, lance corporal."

Jones blushed as he dropped his head. "It was nothing, sir." He still hadn't realized all of what the captain had said.

"Matter of fact," continued the captain, "I understand you've been doing a hell of a job since you got over here."

"Thank you, sir," Jones said modestly.

"Another promotion and you might want to consider eating with us."

"How's that, sir?"

"At the rate you're going, you'll be corporal in another month."

Jones' eyes opened widely again. The expression on his face showed he was baffled.

"You just got promoted to lance corporal," Shaw astutely inserted, realizing Jones hadn't caught on.

"Yeah?" Jones said, looking at the captain and smiling.

"Yes," the captain added as he reached out and firmly shook Jones' hand. "We checked out the area this morning. Charlie was trying to plant some mines on our target range. You probably saved some lives.

Well, that should do it. Your official papers will be handed down today."

The lieutenant and sergeant shook the lance corporal's hand and congratulated him on the promotion which was initiated by Sergeant Webster. When the informal ceremony ended, the officers and sergeant stepped back to their table.

The men at Jones' table were quick to congratulate him. Everybody in the nearly full mess hall would know Lance Corporal Jones by face; at one time or another, they turned and caught the vocal celebration.

But just as abrupt as the rejoicing at the table had begun, it died when Denvo spoke. "Them crackers are something else." Sitting at the table he eyed Jones. "All the shit you done done, you should be corporal anyway." The volume of his voice was low. He shifted his shaded eyes onto everyone at the table, then back to Jones. "If my man here was white, what rank would he be?"

Shaw's reaction to his first taste of black militancy other than that on television (to him television had tended to make issues entertainment rather than realism) was bitterness. *What's wrong with this fool? He's trying to get some shit started, just like H. Rap Brown and Stokely Carmichael.* Shaw's hometown was rather conservative. And blacks were indifferent, or so it seemed, to black militants.

"Don't you think I know it, Denvo," Jones said. "It don't bother me. I'm used to it. It's no different than when I fight a white dude. There ain't too many black judges; I got to win almost every round just to win a split decision. It ain't gonna change."

"It shouldn't be that way," said someone at the table.

Then ice in the canteen holders rattled as the table shook. "It's gonna change or else!" another brother said, using his fist like a hammer to pound the table.

"Yeah," said Navybean, the skinniest dude at the table. "We gotta deal with it, y'all!"

"Cool it, cool it," returned Denvo. "All we got to do is stick together. If something funky goes down, we all go to the old man and demand satisfaction."

"Or else!" the brother said again.

"Or else what?" The sound of impatience was in Denvo's voice as he looked at the brother hard.

The brother, whose face was new to Shaw, reached down and lifted his rifle off the ground. "Some bloodshed," he answered with a sneer, his olive eyes burning with hate. Still looking at Denvo he added, "You supposed to be preaching that, but instead you talkin 'bout begging a white officer."

"You be cool, Milton! I call the shots," explained Denvo. "That's what's wrong with you now—you don't think. Don't you know we outnumbered 6 to 1. We don't intend to start no race riot unless it's the last resort."

Night came quickly for Shaw. Day fragmented as he slept off and on—awake for an hour, asleep for one or two once he awoke for the noon meal. It was 2375. He and Carpenter sat and talked on the hood of the jeep which was parked at guard post #1. The sergeant, Kennedy, had decided he would come on duty at 0200 and relieve Carpenter for the rest of the night.

Guard post #1, facing the main road, reported more sightings of enemy activity than any other. The VC always attempted to mine the road in close proximity to the firebase because an explosion would bottle up outgoing traffic the next morning.

"How you like Boston?" asked Shaw.

"I love it," replied Carpenter. "I've lived there all my life. There's so much going on, and I really miss not seeing baseball."

Shaw's ears caught the way Carpenter pronounced ball. It sounded odd to him.

After a moment of silence Shaw spoke. "What about the Marines?"

"Boy, you change subjects like you're turning the pages of a good novel."

"A lot of things interest me."

"Marines are okay," Carpenter said, nonchalantly. "The Vietnamese say they're dinky dau." He circled his finger at the side of his head as a gesture of what he meant. "I say they're envious of the Army. They're always making remarks about we get anything we want—SP packs, boots, clothes, hardware, you name it. I think their officers feel the same way, too. They're always giving us a bunch a shit about we don't do anything but sleep and lower the morale of their men. Sarge told their captain if he didn't like the way our operation was run, we'd pack up and go back to base camp. Those poor ass bastards don't even have searchlight units. The sarge had the old man by the balls," grinned Carpenter.

Shaw got ready to ask Carpenter about race relations

between black and white Marines, but he stopped short, thinking the question wasn't appropriate.

"No activity at all, yet? This is going to be a quiet night." Carpenter yawned, then flipped his wrist to check the time. He unstrapped the snakeskin band and handed the watch to Shaw. "Wake me up before the sergeant gets here, about ten 'til two, unless something happens. Then wake me up right away."

The next two hours wasn't all lonely or boring for Shaw. Occasionally he chatted with the two Marines in the guard bunker. He listened to the communication checks on the two-way radio lying in the jeep. He started the jeep four and five times an hour, turning on the bright light for two and three minute spells. He observed nothing different, just a green-eyed cat, prancing around outside of the concertina barbed wire.

At 0184 Shaw nudged Carpenter and said, "Wake on up."

The specialist, his 69 inch frame stretched out across the seats in front, lifted an eyelid, then closed it.

Shaw spoke louder. "Didn't you want me to wake you up before the sergeant came?"

"Naw," Carpenter claimed, quickly opening his eyes. "Who cares about him?" He begrudgingly raised his upper body. Then, by holding the steering wheel, he scooted into the driver's seat.

It was 0250 when the sergeant came and relieved Carp.

Boom! Boom! Boom!
The bursts from the cannons woke Shaw. He had

been asleep in the bunker. Light filtered through the passageway. He squinted at the clock on top of Kennedy's foot locker. The short hand was on eight, the long hand on twelve. He had been in the rack only two hours. Now he heard a snore. From the direction it sounded, he knew it was the sergeant.

Boom! Boom! Boom! the cannons spoke again.

The hell with it, Shaw thought, knowing he couldn't turn the noise off. A second later he fell back to sleep.

"What went on with those cannons firing this morning?" Shaw asked as he sat at the chow table with Jones and Denvo. Shaw had had the alarm clock set to ring at noon. With lunch and breakfast being the two hot meals of the day, he always wanted to catch both. He wasn't particularly fond of the C-rats he had to eat for dinner as he ate only bits.

"H and I. Recon spotted signs of a NVA stronghold the other day," answered Jones.

Harassment and interdiction Shaw remembered from AIT (advanced individual training). "What they going to do about the NVA?"

"Nothing, I hope," said the other lance corporal. "Our platoon just left the bush three days ago. Recon's out there now trying to nail down the NVA's strength. If it's only a platoon or two, the 2nd and 4th can take care of business. They're out there somewhere. But more than likely the NVA's at company strength."

Shaw sat erect with his eyes on Denvo. "How long you been in the Nam?"

"A long time, man" he laughed. Then seriousness

echoed in his voice. "I been killing gooks and fighting crackers over here for so long that it seems like years. Eleven months, though."

"I figured you'd been over here for awhile. You seem to know what's happening. How come you only a lance corporal?" It was only equivalent in grade to a PFC in the Army.

"I made corporal in January and got busted down in February."

Shaw waited a couple of seconds to see if Denvo would say why. Shaw knew that he asked a lot of questions, but he couldn't avoid them. The black Marines intrigued him, and he was beginning to sympathize with their militancy in regards to race. Their unity, too, was greater than any he had seen in the Army.

When Denvo continued, Shaw gritted his teeth to keep from smiling. "I drew my rifle on a chuck 90 day wonder who wanted to send my squad on a suicide mission. I commanded all white dudes except one. I told the dumb motherfucker the gooks had retreated too fast; they might be setting up an ambush. He got to talkin about pursue. With my rifle pointing at his gut, I said only if you lead the way." Denvo paused.

"Yeah!" Shaw said, his dark glasses fixed on Denvo's.

Denvo looked at Shaw, probably knowing he had him in suspense. He took a sip of iced tea, then returned. "The chickenshit wonder started talkin about having me court martialed. By then a black gunny sergeant had come up from the rear. He advised the chickshit lieutenant to call in some artillery on the position in the treeline. He did, and I got an article 15.''

"An article 15 for possibly saving a whole squad," Jones voiced in amazement.

"You ain't been over here long enough, Jonesy," added Denvo. "You still got a lot to learn. Shit ain't like you see in Audey Murphy's movies—not for us, anyway." Denvo resumed eating.

"You'll be going home in a month. Won't you, Den?" asked Shaw.

Denvo gulped some tough roast beef and then laughed. "Y'all do 12 month tours. We do 13. I should have joined the Army. Y'all got it made."

The cannons boomed, twenty rounds the first minute.

The men at Shaw's table stared at each other with looks that seemed to say what the hell is going on.

"Now hear this," blasted a voice over the megaphones inside the base. "First and third platoons get prepared for field duty immediately. I repeat . . ."

Before another word resounded out of the megaphones, Denvo spoke. "The shit done hit the fan." His manner was cool. "A company of gooks I bet." He forked in a last bite of food, then stood up. "Later, Army."

Jones stood up, too, and looked at Shaw. "Yeah, brother, we got to make it. I'll see you later."

"Y'all take care now," Shaw closed.

Men scrambled orderly from the mess tent.

Shaw sat there at his empty table, too excited to eat anything else.

A noise different than the persistent boom of the

howitzers got Shaw's attention. It was the sound of helicopters. As the sound came closer, he rose from his cot and stepped out of the bunker. Looking to the blue sky he counted eight helicopters, nearly half the size of Chinooks. Two angled to the ground, whipping up dust and debris. The others hovered at a safe distance overhead. The two helicopters loaded battle-ready Marines, each carrying a rifle, machine gun or grenade launcher. Each also toted a bandolier of ammunition, and hand grenades; some had a LAW. Every Marine wore a flak jacket, helmet, utility belt, and back pack. Soon after the helicopters loaded, they took off, making room for another two to land. The entire lift was completed in ten minutes. As the last helicopter flew off, the base was relieved of noise. The cannons, too, had stopped firing because the copters flew in direction of the mountains.

Later that afternoon Shaw sat inside the puptent with Carpenter and Kennedy as they ate C-rats for dinner. The sides of the tent were rolled completely up. To Shaw, the firebase looked deserted. Most of the remaining men manned the 155s and the guard posts. Four of the six howitzers fired in support of the battle raging at hill six-niner-zero. By now everyone in the base had heard about the 2nd and 4th infantry platoons getting caught in an ambush and losing a third of their men the first hour to a crack NVA company.

"Well," Kennedy said, "Underwood 'll be here tomorrow with the goodies." He grinned, seemingly trying to break the tension.

Carpenter and Shaw remained grim-faced. "The timing couldn't have been better for me," Carpenter said sarcastically. "With thirty-five or forty men in this damn base Charlie might overrun us tonight."

"Cut the shit, Carp," lashed Kennedy. "No sense in you acting like you just came in the country."

"I'm acting like I'm supposed to," Carpenter snapped. "I'm short." He hesitated. "And fuckin right, I'm scared!"

"You're shaking up Jimmy."

"I'm cool, sarge," said Shaw. "If the gooks try to come through that wire, I got something for 'em. I got fourteen extra magazines, all full of ammo. The grunts gave 'em to me."

That night the firebase was under red alert. The Marines popped flares every minute to keep the base lit like daylight.

Charlie never showed.

It was late morning when the three-quarter ton truck marked G/1139th turned from the convoy and into the firebase. A moment later it was parked in front of the Army bunker.

Kennedy stepped out of the bunker. The driver and rider were still in the cab when Kennedy spoke. "Where's Sergeant Underwood?"

Now the other two soldiers had stepped out of the bunker to greet Underwood.

The driver of the vehicle, a gray-eyed staff sergeant, swung the door open, raised his bulky frame from the seat and plodded his way out of the cab. He stared at Kennedy with cold eyes, then finally answered. "He's in the hospital."

"What he do—choke on a fish bone?" Kennedy snickered.

"Watch your jokes," the staff sergeant scolded. "The man damn near didn't make it."

Kennedy's raised cheeks suddenly drooped. "What happened?"

"He caught an AK-47 round in the shoulder. It's shattered to shit."

Shaw frowned, practically feeling the pain. And in disgust he remembered somebody telling him that this was a 'strange mothafuckin war.' Cruel, too, he thought. *Underwood never bothered anybody. He had to be just driving along.* Then Shaw wondered about his own fate. Worried, his hands trembled.

The staff sergeant, Blake his namestrip read, pulled down his jungle shirt. It had tuckered up above his bulging belly. "Who's Carpenter?" he asked.

Carpenter spoke instantly. "I am! I'm packed and ready to go."

"Good. I see you are the Spec 4. We'll be ready to leave just as soon as I get some grub. How's the chow here?"

Carp answered dully. "It's all right."

"They start serving in twenty minutes," Kennedy added, eyeing his wristwatch.

"Well, Sergeant Kennedy, I got your supplies. You can have your men unload."

"I guess I only got one man now."

Shaw was already stepping toward the open bed. Seconds later he stretched his long arms around a box labeled sundry pack. He lifted it out of the bed and staggered with it into the bunker. When he came out, he went to the truck again.

Carpenter commented as Shaw retrieved the case of Cokes. "I might as well stay since we got cigarettes, pop, candy, and a lot of other good stuff." A smile as mischievous as a child's was on his face.

Shaw knew he was only joking.

As Shaw sat on his cot, using his foot locker as a desk, he sealed an envelope. Just moments before he had finished a letter to his mother and brother in which he mentioned that his base provided artillery support for a battle raging tens of miles away. He had exaggerated; the battle was six miles from Mary Ann.

"Ready to go to work, Jimmy? It's just me and you."

Shaw glanced at the alarm clock on top of Kennedy's foot locker. 2200 it read. "Yeah, I feel well rested. I can stay awake 'til morning."

Shaw noted the sergeant never talked much about himself. He decided to find out more about him. "Where you from, sarge?"

"Nashville," the sarge answered concisely, then spoke of the matter ahead. "Well, are you ready?"

Minutes later they set up at guard post #2. They had orders to move to other posts every hour or two.

The red alert had been lifted, and the night, sporadically lit, passed uneventful; a platoon of grunts from another unit had been trucked in during the day.

Br-r-r-r-r..., the alarm clock sounded. Shaw awoke without opening his eyes. He laid there as the clock rang, waiting impatiently for the sergeant to turn off the alarm. Then with the speed of a tortoise

Shaw lifted his eyelids. Afternoon sunlight coming through the passageway illuminated the bunker. His bare eyes blurrily focused on the sergeant's empty bunk. He knew now that it was his duty to deafen the alarm. He wasted no time turning, stretching and then pushing in the stem.

While Shaw dressed, Kennedy walked in the bunker and said, "Those Marines came back from the bush this morning. I was talking with one of the sergeants. He says it was hard going at first. Then artillery softened everything up with direct hits on the reinforced machine gun nests. Artillery's the king of battle." He paused to light-up the pipe he rarely smoked.

Shaw felt better knowing they were back. He thought maybe he had just missed the guys he had gotten acquainted with. "I'm going on to lunch and hear what went on."

Shaw had been sitting at the regular mess table thirty minutes before he saw the Marines that he was most familiar with. It was Denvo and Navybean. They sat down with him, and he smelled the musky odor of the two who hadn't bathed in two days.

Shaw looked at Denvo and thought he looked bad as well as tired. His unshaven face was nubbed with black hairs. His natural was tight and uncombed.

Glancing at Navybean, Shaw noticed a light crease running down his cheek that he hadn't seen before. Although haggard in appearance, Navybean looked better than Denvo.

Again looking at Denvo, Shaw tried to pinpoint what it was that made him appear at least a year older.

"What's happening, y'all," Shaw began.

"You got it," said Denvo. His face brightened with a smile, but it faded quickly.

Navybean already had food in his mouth. He looked at Shaw with dull, listless eyes. He replied by slowly moving his head, up then down.

"Where's Jones?" Shaw asked, looking at Denvo out of his shaded eyes.

Denvo's eyes hid behind dark glasses, too. He squared his face in the direction of Shaw and spoke quietly. "He didn't make it."

Shaw sat still for a second, then returned, "Is he in the hospital or what!"

Perturbed, Denvo screamed, "He got wasted, man!"

Shaw felt his heart sink to the bottom. He closed his eyes in anguish. A vivid picture of a smiling Jones appeared. It's only a dream, he thought—he wished. He opened his moist eyes, wanting to double check with Navybean to see if Denvo was pulling his leg. But then he realized Denvo wouldn't bullshit about a thing like that.

Shaw's hand discreetly moved toward the paper napkins on the table. He fingered one and slid his hand down to his lap. He stood up. "I'm going to get some more lemonade." He turned and walked away, raising the napkin to his eyes as he lifted his sunglasses with the other.

Denvo stared at Shaw's canteen holder still on the table. With Shaw to his back he spoke. "You ain't got nothing to be ashamed of. I cried like a mothafucker. The little nigga was my man." A tear dropped down his cheek.

"Mine, too," said Navybean, nodding back in the chair like he was high.

Denvo returned. "He went down like a hero. But I fault him. It didn't have to happen."

"Yeah," Shaw said softly, turning around. "How did it go down?"

"He was the kind who got carried away in a firefight," said Denvo; "he thought he was invincible. The gook machine guns had us where we couldn't advance. They were firing from pill boxes or something, 200 yards out front. 60mm mortars wouldn't dent their positions. Jones picked up a M-79 grenade launcher from a guy who got hit. I knew what he had in mind. He was going to get close and fire a round through the slits. I told him don't chance it. If I'd still been corporal, I'd ordered him not to. He said don't worry. He started running tree to tree. He got 100 yards. That's where they cut him down. He didn't even have a chance to fire his weapon."

"What are we going to do, pay any respects or anything?"

"I'm going to eat, shave, cold shower, and try to forget about it."

"That's all ya can do, Army," added Navybean, "or shoot some of this good, gook smack I got. Shoot all ya troubles aw-a-a-ay." he ended, his voice fading.

Shaw stood next to the jeep. His eyes followed the intense beam of the searchlight while Kennedy moved it quarter way around the perimeter. "I don't see anything," the sergeant said. "What about you?"

Several seconds passed before the sergeant spoke

again. "Hey, Jimmy!" That caught Shaw's attention; he turned toward the sergeant who continued. "What's wrong with you?"

"Aw, nothing," Shaw answered.

"You seem ill at ease. Maybe even out of it."

Shaw knew what it was: he couldn't get his mind off Jones. And he worried about an identical fate, though he knew he wasn't going to play hero like Jones. He thought about writing Jones' family to tell them he died bravely.

But then he realized he didn't even know Jones' first name.

Kennedy and Shaw awoke the next day, not from the alarm but by a Marine gunnery sergeant shaking Kennedy's cot. The tall, white gunny towered over Kennedy's rack as he said, "I got an order to pass on, Sergeant Kennedy."

"What's that?" Kennedy responded, sitting up in the cot.

"Have you and your man secure your rifles in the arms bunker. The only men allowed to carry rifles inside the base are those on guard duty."

"What!" exclaimed Kennedy, pulling on a pair of trousers. "You got to be kidding. We're in the field. I've heard it done in some units in Da Nang. But here, it's out of the question," he said as he shook his blond head in defiance. "Charlie hear about that, and he'll hit in broad daylight."

"That's why we got guard posts."

"I'm not turning over my weapon or my man's to be locked up!"

"Look Kennedy, I'm trying to be nice. As long

as you're at this base, you know you're under Marine jurisdiction."

Shaw spoke as he sat on the cot. "A good reason's always persuasive, gunny."

Still looking at Kennedy, the gunnery sergeant responded, "I'm not at liberty to say."

"All right, all right," said Kennedy. "We'll turn 'em in as soon as we get dressed. Not too much action at this base no more, anyway."

"Thanks," the Marine said in a pleased tone of voice. He made an about-face and walked out of the bunker.

"You know it's almost lunchtime," said the Army sergeant as he reached for the alarm clock on his foot locker. "We'll turn in our weapons first, then I'm going to find out what's at the bottom of this."

"It don't sound right," added Shaw.

An hour later Shaw sat at his regular mess table. Seven other black enlisted men, all minus weapons, sat close knit around the table. Denvo had informed everyone not to say much, that there would be a meeting in his bunker right after lunch.

Denvo shared his bunker with two other Marines. Photos of young, pretty, black women sat framed on top of two of the foot lockers. The words Bro. Rice were stenciled in black on the other locker. Denvo had folded up his cot to make room for the meeting. He leaned on a green, red, and black flag which draped a large part of the wall behind his rack. For one, the flag was to the black revolutionist what the rebel flag was to the white, Southern conservative: a symbol of racial identity.

Eleven blacks, including Shaw, crammed in the bunker. There were no black officers in the compound; and, except for two high ranking black NCO's, every black was present. "I don't dig this shit—the beast taking our rifles!" someone began in an emotionally charged voice.

"Yeah," someone else added. "What's the deal?"

"Quiet, y'all," Denvo insisted. "Ain't y'all heard what happened in the World?"

"What went down, Denvo?" a low, mean voice demanded.

"The crackers killed King!"

"Martin Luther King?"

"You got it right," Denvo returned forcefully.

The bunker broke into a buzz of revenge: We gotta kick some white ass! We cain't let it go unnoticed. We got to have a day of mourning. Down with the beast!

The news made Shaw's heart ache. *All this killing over here and now Martin Luther King over there. Why?* It greatly disturbed him; and to himself, he prayed for peace.

"That's why the crackers took the rifles!" Denvo yelled. "The brother is rioting in the World, and they know they gonna be doing it here!"

"You damn right!"

"But what we gonna do? The officers got their 45s," Bibbs spoke.

"It don't take a gun to roast one of them smart ass officers," Milton said.

"What you mean?" questioned Bibbs.

Milton was a lance corporal completing his second tour of duty in the Nam. He volunteered for it because he couldn't hack the formalities of stateside duty when he had gone back. He went on to explain. "The officers want to be separate—they shower in different stalls. What we do is pour gasoline in their tank. When the first one of them pulls the shower cord, one of us throws the match."

Nearly everyone looked at Milton strangely.

"Shit, I'll do it!" Milton emphasized.

"Naw, that's too cold," a three striped sergeant said. He was the only sergeant in the bunker.

"Ain't no colder than them blowing King's brains out!" Denvo exclaimed.

Shaw spoke for the first time. "Those were different kinds of people."

"They white. They all think niggas is gonna riot!" exclaimed Milton.

"I ain't going along with roasting nobody," someone said.

Denvo spoke again. "Well, what y'all gonna do? Nothing?"

The sergeant that was tall enough to be a basketball forward squeezed his way to the center. In a low, quiet voice he said, "We gonna see the old man and tell him we want our weapons back 'cause it's not right to assume we gonna riot, and that we want the chaplain to have services for King."

Milton laughed. "You think he's gonna listen to you, nigga?"

"If he don't, I'll personally turn him over and put my lighter to his ass."

"You big enough," Navybean said.

"And ugly enough," someone laughed.

"And black enough," the sergeant added himself.

"And I ain't talkin 'bout color," the dark-skinned Marine clarified.

"Okay, Mike," Denvo conceded, a mischievous grin on his face. "And if he don't listen, how long you gonna hold that lighter to his ass?"

" 'Til he hollers."

Three hours later an order came down that rescinded the earlier order of locking all rifles in the armory. When Shaw heard about this from Sergeant Kennedy, a weak smile flashed across his face. He was sitting on his cot and holding a canteen of water in an unsteady hand.

"You're nervous," Kennedy observed.

Shaw quickly placed the canteen on the ground. "Naw, naw, I'm okay."

"I'm sorry about what happened to Reverend Martin Luther King."

"I am, too. But you don't owe me any apology," Shaw calmly said.

"He never talked about violence. He was opposed to this war. I can't understand why they killed him instead of Stokely Carmichael or that fellow, Malcom X."

"Malcom got it over two years ago," Shaw said slow and blue. "As far as Martin Luther King, it's done. Just like with President Kennedy. He meant a lot to black people, too."

After a brief pause, Shaw finally admitted, "I don't feel so well."

"What's wrong? You down because of Martin Luther King?"

"That's part of it, but mostly I've been jittery

lately. I've lost my appetite. I need to go on sick call tomorrow."

"You can have tonight off. You might feel better tomorrow."

"I don't need to take off. I probably couldn't sleep at night, anyway."

"I got it set up where one of us gets one night off a week. So don't feel like I'm doing you any special favor."

"Okay, in that case, I'll take my night off tonight."

The next morning, not long after a lengthy examination and talk with the corpsman, Shaw placed some personal items inside his backpack. The corpsman had recommended Shaw see an Army psychiatrist. Somewhat like a nurse, a corpsman's medical practice was not too detailed. Sergeant Kennedy had gotten approval from platoon headquarters for Shaw to fly to Qui Nhon, to the closest Army psychiatric unit.

Kennedy poured gasoline into the tank of the jeep as he prepared for the ninety minute drive to Da Nang. From there, Shaw would fly into Qui Nhon. He would have a 24 hour pass.

CHAPTER 6
Qui Nhon

When Shaw stepped off the C-123 airplane at the Qui Nhon airfield, the heat quickly caused him to unfasten another button at the top of his jungle shirt. The tropical temperature, along with the many sunbathers he had seen on the beach while flying in, brought back memories of Cam Ranh Bay, 100 miles south. Now he closely followed the line of men to the terminal. He reached it in two minutes.

Inside the terminal was a bus schedule, posted in the counter area and hung high in a glass casing. The large yellowed lettering contrasted with the charcoal background. A handful of men stood gazing at the schedule, Shaw being the point man. After absorbing some information, he turned and re-checked the wall clock. He determined the bus for him was the 1525. Its destination was the Army hospital.

The gray bus braked gently in front of the hospital gate. The hospital was made up of several large buildings that had the general shape and appearance of housing barracks. The compound was busy, scores of military and civilian personnel shuffling in and out of the buildings. The bus was two-thirds full as the driver opened the door. Moments later he could see only empty seats in his mirror.

As Shaw walked, a sign and arrow led him to his destination. He stepped inside the hospital building, his medical records in hand in a tan folder. He handed them to a young but no so attractive brunette who sat at the desk labeled receptionist. She was dressed in clean, starched jungle utilities, the rank of spec 4 on her upper sleeve. She opened the folder, glanced at the medical records, then told Shaw to have a seat in the corridor.

Nearly a dozen flimsy, plastic chairs lined the corridor where another PFC sat. The sign at the head of the corridor read psychiatric ward. Shaw unshouldered his rifle, removed his backpack and fatigue cap. He then sat down, letting out a sigh.

"Hey, brother," the frail, white PFC said.

Shaw turned his head, and his eyes caught the cloth combat infantry badge and the large 1st Air Cav unit patch on the soldier's uniform. "Yeah?" Shaw responded.

"You got any squares?" He stood up and grimaced.

"Naw."

"Goddamn, I need a smoke." The long, thin soldier held his right leg stiff and limped down the corridor. When he reached one end, he pivoted and started the other way. He stopped in front of the desk and spoke politely. "Have you got a cigarette?"

Their hazel eyes met. "I don't smoke," she replied.

Apparently disturbed, he voiced, "Bitch, I didn't ask you that! I need a square."

"Sir, I'll see if I can find you one." Quickly, she rose to her feet, then in the same manner stepped through an open door. Seconds later, she returned, and a mustached captain in a long, white coat accompanied her. "He's the one," she yelled, pointing at the white PFC while he stood waiting at the desk.

As she had yelled, the PFC had spun like a running

back, almost as if he had forgotten about his bad leg. His eyes went wild with rage. "Ugly bitch, what you done told the doctor?"

Like calming a barking dog, the doctor said, "It's all right, soldier. She just told me you needed a cigarette," he cleverly continued. He reached in the lower pocket of his white, medical coat and pulled out a pack of Kools. "You smoke this kind?"

The expression of the PFC's face softened with delight. "They'll do," he played it down. "Salem's my brand."

"Come on in my office," the captain said stepping forward and then placing his arm gently around the PFC's shoulder. Let's talk about what you're here to see me for."

The PFC turned his head toward Shaw, winked and said, "They all think I'm crazy. But not me."

Shaw just wondered. He figured a little acting could be involved, especially after the wink. Then that idea came back. *If it can get me home, I'm going to do the same thing.* Just then he heard the door to the medical captain's door close.

A half an hour later the PFC was escorted out of the office, down the corridor and around the corner by the captain.

Five minutes later the captain returned, alone. He stopped at the desk, chatted with the spec 4 and then lifted Shaw's medical records from the desk top. He opened the folder and read what little information the corpsman had scribbled. Closing the folder, he turned and faced Shaw, then spoke. "Come on in my office, Jim."

Shaw stood up and followed the captain into the

office of neatly shelved medical journals and plush furnishings.

The captain moved to the swivel chair behind his glass-topped, walnut desk and sat down. Captain Matthew H. Delph, MD was engraved in a walnut-stained inkpen block. It sat atop the desk within reach of the captain's right hand. "Have a seat," he told Shaw.

The thick cushion of the fabric chair at the side of the desk sank slowly but not too deeply. "This is a comfortable chair, sir. You have it shipped in from the States?"

"Something like that." Then he pulled a sheet of stationery in front of him and removed one of the two pens from the holder. "Okay, Jim, what makes you think you need my help?"

"The medic's the one who advised me to seek psychiatric help," Shaw replied in a serious tone.

"Oh yes," said the psychiatrist, "he did write in your record that your problem of no appetite and nervousness could be more psychological than physical. He says there's no sign of ulcers. Your temperature and blood pressure were normal, and your weight is 143. How much did you weigh when you left the States last month?"

"150," he exaggerated.

"Exactly 150?"

"Maybe 148."

"I see," the captain said, then hesitated a few seconds. "Are you taking malaria pills?"

"Right."

"Do they make your bowels run?"

"Sir, I've been through all that with the medic,"

Shaw said, seemingly irritated. "They don't bother me."

"So you seem to think everything is psychological, too?"

"I don't know," snapped Shaw. "That's why I'm here."

"Back home does your family or a girlfriend have any pressing problems—illnesses, recent deaths, financial problems—those sort of things?"

"Nothing new."

"What's old then?"

"Well, my old man drinks a lot. He's caused my mother a lot of hardships—to work two part-time jobs, to worry a lot, being separated. Stuff like that."

"Does your father's drinking disturb you?"

"I'm used to it," Shaw said, not directly answering the question. The more he talked or thought about it, the more it disturbed him. "But he's beautiful when he's not drinking."

"I see, and do you drink?"

"A little."

"Is there any record of mental instability in your family?"

"An uncle," Shaw lied, assuming it could be linked hereditarily.

"Whose side?"

"My father's, naturally."

The captain looked Shaw stern in the face as he spoke again. "That's strange—one's an alcoholic and the other's mentally ill."

Beads of sweat popped out on Shaw's forehead. "Well, it's true."

"I never said it wasn't," the captain returned with a straight face.

The psychiatrist continued his interrogation into Shaw's background for forty-five minutes, trying to diagnose any mental illness. At the end, his conclusion was frank. "Jim, you're as sane as I am. What you seem to be suffering from is a mild form of anxiety, bringing on some nervous tension. It only tells me you're sound psychologically. What field soldier wouldn't fear for his life or be shook by the dreadful things happening around him? Just some. I think as time goes by, most of that fear will dissolve."

"You mean the things happening around me, I'll get used to."

"Well put, Jim. But your biggest fear or worry seems to be about home. I'll prescribe a tranquilizer, librium. It will help."

Shaw spoke strongly. "But I think there's more to it. I've been suffering at night with horrible dreams..."

The psychiatrist raised his voice. "You think you're insane, don't you?"

Shaw sat quiet, not knowing how to answer the question. If he said no, all hope of being sent home would be gone. If he said yes, and the doctor believed him, he didn't want a section 8 discharge.

Shaw was naive, thinking it would be that simple getting out of the Army, or for that matter, Vietnam.

Seconds passed while Shaw tried to decide on which way to answer, but the captain interrupted. "Come with me. I want to show you something."

Both men walked out of the office, down the corridor and into a room with two beds. A white, cloth partition divided the room. A soldier, being consoled by a Vietnamese nurse, laid in one of the beds. The other bed was empty.

"Now let's just wait here a moment," the captain whispered to Shaw.

"You brave man, Sergeant James," the nurse said, trying to calm the soldier as he twisted and turned.

The soldier screamed. "That damn CO got us all killed! He did! He did!" His eyes were closed.

"It okay now," said the nurse, adjusting the reddened bandage around his head. "You go home when you get better."

"The whole platoon!" he cried. "Jake! Roger! Craig! Joe! Tex! Everybody!"

Obviously touched, Shaw turned his head, looked down and backed out the door.

"That's just the first one. You want to see others?" asked the captain.

"Not really. I see what you're trying to tell me. What happened to that guy who talked to you before I did?"

"Oh, him. He's gone. Mentally, I mean. But he doesn't think he is. Usually, that's the way it is. I think he had problems before he joined the Army He said he joined so he could come over here and fight. And be a hero. He's just a poor, neglected Tennessean Appalachian."

"Where you from, sir?"

"Brooklyn. Well, since you'll be here until tomorrow, enjoy yourself. I'll get your prescription and have your records mailed back, SOP here. You said you play piano. There's one in the dayroom in Alpha building."

"Yeah!"

Two soldiers sat reading in the large room where the ebony, baby grand piano matched the paint of the wall bookshelf. Shaw strolled into the room. Then, disregarding the men, pool table, books, and magazines, he stepped toward the piano. Quickly there, he pulled the stool and eased down. He pushed the piano cover back. Looking at the keys, he could hear the tone to each one. With his right hand, he ran up the scale on the white keys, instantly detecting that the piano was out of tune, lowered by half a pitch. Not much of a problem, he thought.

"Hey, hey, we're trying to read in here," one of the soldiers complained. He was a middle-aged staff sergeant.

Shaw ignored him, knowing he had to play and how he had to do it. The ballad *Stardust* entered his mind. A pretty song, he thought, that would ease the pain of being in the Nam. The fingers on his right hand smoothly ran off the melody, and his left hand moved in a chopping motion, bringing out the harmony and rhythm. His sound was modern.

"Hey, why didn't you tell me you could play Hoagy Carmichael?" the sergeant returned, politely.

Shaw was halfway through the song when the other soldier closed his book, sat back and shut his eyes.

The sound of more than two pairs of clapping hands filled the room when Shaw finished the song; his audience had doubled.

"You a jazz player?" asked the black soldier with Williams printed on his namestrip.

"I play it all," boasted Shaw as he was intoxicated with delight. "Gospel, jazz, pop, a little classical. And I play 'em good, too!"

"If you're going to be here long, I'll go get my man. He plays jazz sax."

"Go get him!" Shaw urged with a robust smile. "I'll be here!"

Williams briskly stepped out of the room.

Then the staff sergeant spoke again. "Do you know *April in Paris?*"

"Aw, yeah," Shaw answered brightly.

"I go back to the big band era."

"That was a creative period. I'll play some Duke Ellington things, too."

First Shaw counted off a medium, swing temp for *April in Paris*. Half a minute later he was through the head. When he got into the improvisation, he noticed everybody was tapping their feet along with his. It made him feel good, and he reached down for something extra, causing the staff sergeant to hum on the chord changes.

As the last note faded, applause abruptly echoed across the room. Shaw responded with a smile and nod, like he had many times before in dance hall gigs back home.

Alone, Second Lieutenant Williams re-entered the dayroom. By the slight frown on the young lieutenant's face, Shaw was convinced the lieutenant's friend couldn't be found.

"That's all right," Shaw said as Williams stepped closer, "I'll be here after dinner."

Williams shrugged his shoulders in disappointment. "Sorry, man, he won't be back until Saturday."

That was two days away, and Shaw knew he had to fly back tomorrow.

CHAPTER 7
Con Lo

The return flight found Shaw in a Chinook. It was the only direct flight of the morning. The long-bodied chopter was closing in on the landing pad as it flew over Marble Mountain. The hugh mountain overlooked the large military base at the seaport city of Da Nang.

But, suddenly, Shaw felt heavy thuds and heard loud bangs in the body of the helicopter.

"Antiaircraft fire!" yelled one of the helmeted gunners. Then he let loose with the M-60. The red tracers drew a bowed line, but the experienced gunner guided it straight to the mark, where he had seen flashes of muzzle fire high on the side of the mountain.

The military passengers, locked in by seat belts, curled—making their bodies as small as possible.

But the helicopter itself was the target. Well aimed shots with armor piercing rounds ruptured the engine, which smoked, sputtered and then choked. The blades coasted to a stop. Now that the helicopter had just cleared the mountain, the ground was 2,000 feet below. The helicopter spun and dropped. Only a matter of seconds brought it 1,000 feet closer to the ground.

Shaw's heart thumped and pounded. With his eyes involuntarily closed, his childhood raced across his mind. Vivid pictures of the happier and sadder moments flipped by like frames in a slide projector, tens of frames a second.

Then, as if a prayer answered, the fall of the helicopter was broken by a jolt. The blades began to spin at half speed, stabilizing the craft.

Several seconds later the captain spoke over the intercom, sheer excitement and delight in his voice. "We're under control now! Dammit! We're under control! But stay in your seat belts! We'll have to coast down, and there's no telling where we'll land!"

Now at six hundred feet the craft fell gracefully like a falcon on a downward glide. The half speed of the blades provided only some lift. Three hundred feet from the ground, the pilot revved the engine as much as possible, increasing the speed of the blades and the lift of the craft. It finally touched down, the impact only a degree more than a parachutist would sustain. The landing pad was solid ground on the side of a hill.

In five minutes rescue vehicles, sirens blasting, ascended on the tilted aircraft and found it already deboarded.

"I thought I was through," a jubilant Shaw told Sergeant Kennedy as they rode back to Mary Ann in the jeep. "Never been so scared in my life. I know what it feels like now to be scared stiff; I had no body control at all."

"For everybody's sake on that chopper, I'm glad you all landed safely," said Kennedy.

"They'll have to salvage that copter. It was shot up pretty bad."

"I know that hurts the Army," the sergeant said

sarcastically. "They treasure equipment more than they do a few pions."

Kennedy's comment strangely enough made Shaw feel more comfortable. *He's regular. He ain't no fool that believes the Army can do no wrong.* Shaw asked, "Since you're a sergeant, you gonna make a career out of the Army?"

"Who, me?" the sergeant laughed. "I joined the Army so I could travel—see the world. That was in '62. In '65 I re-upped for three more, for the same reason. Besides going almost everywhere in the States, I had tours in Germany and Korea. I was supposed to go to Panama, but then they changed my orders and shipped me to this shithole over here." Emphatically he ended, "This is my last year in the Army!"

The Army'll fuck anybody, black or white. Or as the drill sergeants said, 'We treat everybody the same.'

Silence fell between the two as Kennedy eyed the road and steered the jeep. But the silence was only momentary. Kennedy broke it. "How'd that appointment with the doctor go?"

"All right. He gave me a tranquilizer. I feel better already. It relaxes me."

"You'll need it after this morning, won't you?" said the sergeant, his face slightly contorted by a smirk.

Shaw cracked no smile. *If only he'd been in my shoes.* "That shit was serious this morning!"

"Sorry about that," Kennedy apologized as the smirk disappeared. "The way you were talking about it, I didn't know you took it that serious." He paused. "Well, we'll be moving to another location next week. North, about ten miles to work with a CAC unit, or is it CAG unit."

"What's that?"

"Combined Action Group. A small group of Marines working in a ville with a group of local South Vietnamese Army Regulars."

"That sounds interesting."

"It sounds scary to me. I don't trust any Vietnamese that's got a weapon."

"I really mean about working in the ville."

Kennedy's bluish eyes seem to brighten. "Oh, yeah, if the skivvy houses got any decent girls, it 'll be interesting!"

Eight days later Kennedy and Shaw left Firebase Mary Ann. It was 1350 when the jeep hit Route 1. Every inch of cord that ran through the border of the canopy cover on the trailer was extended to hold in the full load.

Twenty minutes later Kennedy slowed at a side road while Shaw read the map. "This should be Con Lo," stated Shaw.

Kennedy made a 90° turn. As he drove further in on the side road, he saw the shabby dwellings; "That's got to be it, Jimmy."

"Yep. Tacky, like all the rest."

The size and appearance of the village was typical of those in the northern sector of South Vietnam. On each side of the narrow dirt road a dozen closely spaced square huts made up the central sector of the village. Other huts, scattered a mile down Route 1, were like a suburb. The huts were assembled with anything the Vietnamese builder was able to gather—

bamboo and thatch for awnings, scraps of plywood and sheet metal for the roofs and sidings, flattened aluminum cans and 2 by 4s for the doors. The huts bore no glass windows; instead, sections were cut out of the sides, lifted on hinges and held in place by 2 by 4s.

As they reached the village, Shaw smelled an odor, not foul but pungent. Yet, it nearly turned his stomach. Vietnamese cooking, he figured, because he did smell some fish.

The jeep crept along, Shaw and Kennedy taking in the sights, when an underfed kid ran to the passenger side. He trotted with the vehicle. Then he stuck out his bony arm, the diameter that of a mop stick. He displayed a forearm of wristwatches. "You like Seiko?" the kid perhaps twelve-years-old, asked.

Shaw eyed the watches with interest.

Looking at Shaw the kid said, "Soul, you #1. I sale you Seiko for 20 MPC."

"Didi mau," Kennedy said angrily to the kid.

The kid ignored the sergeant and quickly said, "15 MPC."

Fifteen dollars, Shaw thought; not bad. Just then his head snapped back; Kennedy had accelerated. The jeep began speeding away, stirring dust. Shaw twisted a slightly stiff neck and stared, bewildered, at the sergeant.

"Don't buy anything from these Vietnamese children," insisted Kennedy. "As innocent as they look, they're con artists. They get those $3 Sieko watches, somehow transpose the i and e, and try to pass them off as real Seikos. You can get a real one—I mean real—at the PX for $39.95."

The jeep slowed again at the end of the road. Several tents and a few bunkers inside concertina barbed wire ran perpendicular to the road. The Republic of South Vietnam flag flew high on one side of the compound; the American flag on the other.

After staking their tent, Kennedy and Shaw rechecked with the three-striped sergeant who was the highest ranking Marine in the compound. He commanded two squads. "Is there any way we can get a phone wired up in our tent?" asked Kennedy.

An inch shorter in height, the chubby Marine sergeant faced Kennedy and stood close. The Marine's face was close shaven, round at the cheeks and chin. His thick, sandy mustache seemed to add maturity to his face. Being economical with his words he said, "We don't run phones here—too small."

As they stood in the commo and command post tent, Shaw glanced at the bulky master transmitter-receiver that sat on the table desk. Kennedy glanced at the smaller two-way radios on the ground and asked, "What about a radio? We'll need one to make our checks and monitor what's happening."

The Marine sergeant bent down, then lifted the radio pack by one of its back straps. He handed the radio to Kennedy, told him what frequency to set it on and what his call sign would be.

Shaw dipped his metal eating utensils, that hung on a foot of twine, in sudsy, boiling water to clean them. He had already scraped the plate. Then he dipped the utensils in clear, boiling water to rinse them. They air dried as he walked back to the tent.

He had just finished dinner. The hot meal had been driven in from Marine regiment headquarters, four miles north and half a mile east.

Kennedy was sitting on his cot reading when Shaw entered. Kennedy laid down the eight day old *Playboy* magazine which he had bought at the PX in Da Nang. He spoke. "Let's go to the ville."

"Yeah, anything beats just sitting around here."

Each soldier shouldered his rifle, and in just utilities, cap, and boots they marched the 150 yards into the village.

The pungent odor hit Shaw again. He sniffed while turning his head, learning that the odor came from no specific direction. Then he looked around the ville at the lack of anything modern or fashionable. A century behind, he estimated modestly.

The villagers were friendly. Old men standing here and there with their hands clasped in front of them smiled and nodded as the two soldiers passed. Snow white hair, like thick strands of silk, fell from the chins of the old men, down to their chests. Most of the older women who smiled displayed unattractive, darkened teeth. Shaw thought sadly that they each had a mouth full of decayed teeth, until Sergeant Kennedy indicated it was customary for those women to stain their teeth with beetlenut. The attractive, younger women generally had half smiles on their faces. They wore gowns over their standard loose black pants. These light and pastel colored gowns, called ao dais, were full length and split to the waist on both sides. They appeared to open like butterflies when blown by a breeze. The little children played with Shaw and Kennedy from a distance by making faces and sticking out their tongues, and they always managed to say something like 'me joke with you' or 'you #1' at the end of their playful mischief.

Kennedy and Shaw stopped in front of a hut that had fruit—melons, bananas and oranges—displayed in a rusty metal bin. Half a dozen small, wooden tables were under the awning of the hut. Soiled beige linen covered the tables. "I'm going to sit down and have a Coke," said Kennedy as he eyed the Coca Cola bottles sitting in a bin of water next to the fruit bin.

He and Shaw sat down.

"May I help you?" a young, Vietnamese woman said. Long, black hair fell down the back of her canary yellow ao dai. She wore white, satin pants. There was nothing tight about them.

"Two cokes," answered Kennedy.

A moment later the waitress in yellow returned with two opened bottles of Coke. "30 piasters," she said, placing the bottles on the table.

Kennedy removed his wallet from his hip pocket and took it out of a waterproof—plastic—envelope. He pulled out a MPC with a 1 on it. It was the equivalent of a dollar in American money and 40 piasters in Vietnamese money. "Keep the change," he said, handing the waitress the orange colored paper money. It was just a tab smaller than a dollar bill.

"Thank you," the woman said with a bow.

Shaw placed his hands around the cool, wet bottle, raised it to his mouth, and took a sip. It didn't have enough carbonation in it, he immediately tasted. He sat the bottle down and accidentally saw the word

Saigon at the base. He assumed the pop was bottled there, and now he had second thoughts about drinking any more. He feared Nam's sanitary standards would be far below those in the States. And he had been told at his Vietnam briefing not to drink any of their water without first boiling it or using a purification tablet.

After the sergeant drank his Coke, he ordered and paid for a cantaloupe. He ate the large sized melon more like he was starved than hungry. He finished, looked at Shaw and asked, "When you gonna finish your Coke?"

"I'm not. It was bottled here."

"It's okay. I drink 'em all the time."

"Naw. I'll pass."

"You gonna turn down one of them young whores, too, 'cause she might not be clean?"

Shaw grinned. "If she looks good enough, I'll just have to use a rubber." He had been told, too, about the high number of VD cases, particularly gonorrhea. One medical captain had even claimed that certain strains of asian gonorrhea and malaria could render recipients sterile, possibly for life. He stressed using prophylactics when applicable and taking malaria pills regularly.

"Aw, come on," Kennedy frowned. "I've never used anything. And never caught the claps."

Shaw's eyes opened wider. "Really?" He wasn't fond of latex, anyway.

"I'm not putting you on," said Kennedy, a sincere look on his face.

Shaw made no comment.

The sergeant stood and motioned the waitress.

When she came to the table, he asked in a whisper, "You boom boom girl?"

The young lady showed no sign of being offended. It was a good indication that she was a prostitute or she was used to answering the question by American servicemen mistaking her for one or willing to make her one. She looked straight ahead and pointed to a hut at the end of the village. "You go see mama-son. She got girls you pay for."

"Thanks," the sergeant said, his manner congenial. "Come on, Jimmy. Let's see what the skivvey house in the ville's about."

Shaw rose lazily as usual and followed Kennedy to the hut the waitress had pointed out.

The door to the hut was wide open. The two stepped inside. The wide front room was lit only by shadowed evening light coming in the front door.

A lady who looked to be fifty years old was the first to greet them. "I know you not been here before. We have pretty girls. You sit down and wait. They come." She walked out of the front room toward the back.

As Kennedy and Shaw sat down, the legs of the wooden stools nudged into the ground a bit. Soon, a young woman appeared and sat next to Kennedy. She wore loose, black, satin pants and a loose white blouse. Shaw was disappointed that she wore nothing to reveal how shapely her legs or body was. And he thought she looked too young for him. Fifteen or sixteen, he guessed.

Once Shaw's shaded eyes adjusted to the dimly lit room, he saw a Marine sitting on the other side, being corraled by a young woman who had her arms around him.

"Kim busy," the woman said to the Marine. "You take me, huh, huh?" She spoke softly while trying to kiss the Marine on his ear.

"I want Choi then," the Marine said, pushing the woman away with his muscular, sun-tanned arms. He was wearing a green T-shirt. "You tell mama-son Kim or Choi, or I no fuck!"

The woman got up, seemingly frustrated, and ran through the orange curtain which divided the front and back rooms.

A few seconds later mama-son re-entered the front with a smile. Her teeth were free of beetlenut stain. "Kim very busy," she said, looking at the Marine. "You wait on Choi? She almost fini." Mama-son's mechanical, English monologue was supplemented with a French word here and there.

Shaw, like the majority of American servicemen, knew little about Vietnamese history or culture. He never knew the French occupied South Vietnamese soil as allies through the mid '50s.

"Me no wait!" screamed the Marine, emulating the English of mama-son so she could understand him, without him repeating. Then he calmly left the hutch.

Out of the corner of his eye Shaw saw Kennedy stand up and give the old lady some money as she had stepped to their area. Kennedy then followed the very young woman through the orange curtain divider.

The girl who had been trying to coax the Marine stepped back into the front room. She gave a sultry look to Shaw. Her big, brown eyes seemed to glow, and she moistened her ruby-ed lips with her tongue. She slowly approached Shaw, her narrow hips switching side to side. "Soul brother, you like me?" she asked romantically as she stepped close.

Her short cut black hair didn't seem to do much for her in Shaw's opinion. She was also too pale and not that cute. He said, "I'm waiting on my friend."

She looked at Shaw curiously, her head tilted.

He thought maybe she didn't understand. "I, he pointed at himself, then proceeded deliberately with the sentence, "am waiting on the sergeant. I am not a customer."

"Bullshit, Soul," she burst quickly, a frown now on her face. "You want other girl. You #10."

Shaw sat calm while the young woman, not able to turn a trick, stormed outside. Then to Shaw's surprise a Marine lieutenant emerged from the back. He walked straight out the front door, a healthy grin on his face.

Shit, he's human.

A second later another young woman and mama-son walked through the curtain. Mama-son in her green ao dai and wooden sandals spoke to Shaw. "This is pretty lady, Choi." Mama-son held the very attractive young woman by the arm. "She can make soul brother very happy. She my #1 girl. She cost you twice as much—10 MPC."

The young woman stared at Shaw, displaying no signs of emotion. She bowed down, and her long, raven black hair fell to the front. She raised, and it neatly went back in place down her back.

Shaw could not take his eyes off the young woman. He always had a passion for women with beautiful, black hair, particularly if it was long. That alone would have made him stare at her, but the curl of her thin lips, the baby smoothness of her yellowish complexion, the sweet scent of her perfume, and the delicate way she carried herself made him want her. He stood up, his rifle still on his shoulder, and removed his wallet. He fumbled through the ones and fives. Then he pulled out the single ten. Anxiously, he handed mama-son the military payment certificate.

Choi expressed her first emotion in regards to Shaw. She smiled. She revealed a close-spaced, decayless set of teeth, though more yellow than white. "Come with me," she spoke gently.

Shaw followed her into the back, past four other rooms shielded with curtains. She pulled back the curtain on the last room and waved Shaw in.

The dull, little room had a wooden bed. The mattress was a layer of blankets. A burning candle lit the room, and burning incense deodorized it. A pan of water sat on a crate.

Shaw unshouldered his weapon, and before he could do anything else, Choi let her one-piece red pajama-like outfit fall to the matted floor. She was shapely: 34-22-33.

Quickly he removed his uniform and underwear. Then he pulled the sparsely haired, petite woman to the bed. He used no protection, knowing she was just as pure and clean inside as she was outside.

The Army team stationed its searchlight on a ridge at the back of the CAC compound. Below the ridge was a valley. Past the five hundred foot clearing, a jungle of trees reached the hills two miles to the west. The radio pack sat in the front seat of the jeep. Kennedy and Shaw stood at the rear, scanning an 180° area with the searchlight. They scanned every half hour or so. They used the white beam since it had more depth.

At 2375 a call came over the radio for Firebase Carol. Carol was three miles away. The call was from the CAC night patrol. They called for illumination rounds.

At 2380 an illumination round burst brilliantly two miles to the south. Other than that the night passed uneventfully.

The next few nights passed virtually the same, making Kennedy and Shaw so complacent that they began sleeping more than working.

However, the days were different. Kennedy visited the ville daily like it was home. But Shaw stayed around the compound. There was nothing much in the ville for him. Not even Choi since he had painfully discovered upon urinating that she had given him the clap. Two shots of penicillin had cured the disease, but the thought of his manhood behaving like a running nose was a turn-off.

Writing letters to home, reading whatever was available, or talking with Marines occupied Shaw most of the time.

The tranquilizers had slowed him down and his appetite had returned. He had ballooned to 156, but it was not all around his waist.

One day, finally, there was a mail call for Shaw. Staff Sergeant Blake had driven in from base camp to hand him five letters, postmarked in April. It was now May. The first letter he hastily opened was from his mother. Good news kept him smiling through both pages. The second letter he opened was from his girlfriend. The smile remained. The letters from Joey, his father, and a friend kept him smiling, also.

Then that evening, as he sat across the dinner table from Kennedy, Shaw spoke. "You been getting much mail?"

"Not much," answered Kennedy. The fact didn't seem to bother him; no frown was visible. "My mom's not living. My older brother and dad write sometimes, and I write them."

"What about your girl?"

"I didn't leave any in the States. I'm glad I didn't in a way. I'll have no guilty conscience."

Shaw stopped eating. He looked the sergeant in the eye, not sure why he said that.

"I asked Le to marry me," explained the sergeant. "She agreed. I'm going to send her to the States. I told Sergeant Blake this afternoon so he can help me get her expedition papers."

Shaw sat stunned and disappointed. He knew Kennedy had only been seeing the girl three weeks, and he thought Kennedy was more selective than to choose a village prostitute—an average looking one at that. He remembered her as the fifteen or sixteen year old girl that Kennedy first went to bed with. Shaw wondered how long the sergeant would stay with the girl once he took her back to the States and started looking at those tall, mature, fine, meaty American women.

"I know you, sarge. Are you sure you're not just

feeling sorry for her 'cause she's so young and doing what she's doing?"

"She's very sweet. We're in love."

Sarge don't do nothing! Gets a little trim and falls in love. I thought he could handle his self.

Disgusted, Shaw spoke loudly as he tried to rock some sense into the sergeant. "But you still got five more months to do over here. Things might change!"

"When she gets her papers in order, I'm going to send her home to stay with my dad."

"Suppose you get wasted!"

Kennedy's eyes opened widely. He was speechless for a second. It was as if he had never thought of it until now. "Maybe we'd better leave the Nam together," he answered meekly.

"Yeah."

The next day Shaw sat in a tent with two black Marines. "You the coolest motherfucker I done ever seen," said one of the Marines. "Ain't he, Rob?"

The Marine named Rob laughed, turning his head toward Shaw. "Yeah. He called it right. I ain't never seen you hurry to do nothing or get excited in them shades."

Shaw cracked a smile and said, "Y'all crazy."

"Coolbreeze. That's it! That's what I'm gonna call you," laughed Rob.

The days in May had been reaching the upper 80's, dropping moderately to the lower 70's at night. Nightly rain fell, and sun shine days enhanced the growth of the vegetation, which shot up, reminding Shaw of the time a drill instructor spoke of how fast things grew. The instructor had said the VC make prisoners talk by taking them out to a young bamboo field and staking them tight to the ground of a cut out area. In a day the bamboo would grow enough to pierce the body of the captives as they screamed out information. Shaw always wondered if that actually happened, knowing the DI thought little of surrender.

Four days had passed when Sergeant Blake returned.

He sat on a folding wooden chair inside his men's tent.

Kennedy, looking at Blake's striped upper sleeve, remarked, "Hey, when'd you make platoon sergeant?"

Blake's plump jaws shifted upward when he smiled. "Just the other day. Hell, I been doing the job ever since Underwood got hit."

Immediately that got Shaw's attention. He placed the letter he was reading on the cot. It had been brought in by Blake. "You heard from him?"

"He's doing fine. He sent the lieutenant a letter. He's home now."

"Glad to hear that," Shaw returned, his tone of voice bright.

Blake's plump jaws slipped down as he eyed Kennedy. "I got some not so good news."

Kennedy straightened up in his chair and gave Blake a serious stare.

The platoon sergeant continued. "You're getting transferred to the 4th platoon."

"But that's in Chu Lai," said Kennedy, amazement on his face.

"Be ready to pull out of here Friday."

"And that's only two days from now!" The sergeant paused, then asked less vocal, "Well, did you get those visa papers?"

"The lieutenant wants you to drop that. He says there's too many complications involved."

"Fuck him!" Kennedy screamed as he stood up. "I'll go see the old man in Phu Bai."

"I wouldn't be surprised if that's where it came from, headquarters," returned Blake. "There's too many guys deserting Vietnamese women in the States. That's not necessarily saying you might do it. There's just a move to discourage guys from marrying these women until after they've been home on leave and thought things over."

"Then I can fly back here on my own, take her back and marry her?" Kennedy said sarcastically.

"Something like that, Bill."

"Dammit! That's shit!" said Kennedy, pacing the tent. "Who can afford to fly back to this shithole!"

"I know how you must feel. Just calm down."

"You don't know nothing about feeling, Blake!" Kennedy stood in one spot for a moment, appearing to be in a daydream. Then he spoke with less emotion. "Is Jimmy going with me?"

"No. Just you. Actually, you're getting more responsibility. You'll be in charge of two searchlights and four men."

Shaw entered the conversation. "Where am I going then, Sergeant Blake?"

"You're going to be part of a three man crew. Sergeant McHale is coming down from Phu Bai tomorrow, and I'm bringing in a new man from base camp."

"Where's our man?" asked Kennedy the next day,

checking his wristwatch. It read one o'clock.

"Yeah, he should have been here by now if he was coming by convoy," returned Shaw, sitting in the tent, sheltered from the drizzle.

An hour later an Army jeep marked G/1139th pulled into the CAC compound. "Hey, sarge," said Shaw, looking out the open side of the tent, "there's a brand new searchlight just drove in."

Kennedy jumped up and looked out. "That's got to be McHale." He stepped outside and yelled, "Over here."

The lone occupant of the jeep turned his head toward the voice. The soldier's sleepy brown eyes appeared to awaken; quickly they opened fully. The brown hair under his helmet was straight and short. He arm wrestled with the steering wheel until he had the jeep turned around. Then he drove to the tent and parked. A few seconds later he was out of the vehicle. And he stretched.

"You must be Sergeant McHale," Kennedy said, approaching the medium built soldier with his hand open and arm extended.

"Yeah, yeah," the soldier said through a broad smile. His gapped teeth were solid white, and he talked country. Regular sergeant stripes and the lips-shaped 1139th Artillery patch with two cannon barrels crossed over the top of a skull—*the kiss of death*—decorated the shoulders of his utilities.

Rain dampened Kennedy's hair as he shook hands with McHale. "Come on in." They stepped inside the 18 by 24 foot tent, and Kennedy continued, "How was your ride?"

"Long. Started out at nine. The convoy didn't

get movin 'til almost ten-thirty. Sappers blew a culvert eight miles outside Phu Bai."

Kennedy motioned McHale towards Shaw. "I want you to meet PFC Jimmy Shaw."

McHale shook Shaw's hand. "Howd'y."

Shaw nodded, no readable expression on his face.

"Jimmy's a good man, sergeant." Then a smirk appeared on Kennedy's face. "He don't drink, smoke or screw. But he curses like hell."

Looking at Kennedy and smiling, Shaw spoke. "Come on, sarge. Don't kid him like that. He might think I'm square." Shaw turned his head toward McHale. "He's just exaggerating."

Still, grinning, McHale added, "I cain't afford to believe everthing I hear."

"Where you from, Mac?" asked Kennedy.

"Fort Worth," McHale said, turning and facing Kennedy, "and Mac's what they call me down home, but only it's Little Mac. Pa's Big Mac."

For ninety minutes Kennedy continued a conversation with the other sergeant, mostly briefing him about the job, the Marines, and why he was getting transferred.

Then they ate dinner, and afterwards they slept.

That night the three men worked continuously—something Kennedy and Shaw hadn't done in weeks. Shaw knew it was to impress the new man; no enemy activity had been reported since their first night there. And many Marines said it was due to the presence of the searchlight.

1325 the next day, Sergeant Blake drove into the compound. He had flowed with the regular light traffic and avoided the morning convoy. The compound had just finished serving lunch. It was like the big man had missed the meal on purpose; he had complained to Kennedy about his surging weight the last time. Blake parked his three-quarter ton behind the jeeps. He and a Puerto Rican PFC whose namestrip spelled Figuero stepped from the cab. They were welcomed by the other three soldiers right outside the tent.

"I'm ready to go," Kennedy said somberly. "I talked everything over with Le early this morning. She didn't even seem to care—I mean she didn't seem disappointed I got transferred. She seemed to worry about whether or not I was going to send her to the States. So I told her let's forget everything, like Jimmy had said." With his head down he slowly went inside the tent and came back out with his foot locker.

"Load it in the new jeep," instructed Blake. "You're driving it down to Chu Lai after a night in Da Nang."

Half-an-hour later Kennedy's vehicle followed Blake's out of the compound.

"Well," said Shaw sitting in the tent with McHale and Figuero, "maybe the transfer was a blessing in disguise for Sergeant Kennedy. I sure hated to see him go, though; he was all right."

"The Army knows what they're doing," McHale said. "They run into situations like that all the time."

Shaw suddenly became wary of McHale. *I bet this guy's a lifer.*

Shifting his eyes to the straight haired Figuero, Shaw asked, "What do you think about it?"

With the exception of his non-Oriental eyes and American uniform, Figuero resembled a young Vietnamese soldier. He was small in stature and had yellowish-tan skin. "You speak too fast," he said slowly himself. He had a dense Latin accent. "I do not understand English too good."

"I know better," said Shaw. All the Puerto Ricans he had encountered in the Army were from New York and always pretended not to understand something when they didn't want to give an answer. "You from New York?"

"No. San Juan."

"Puerto Rico!"

"Yes."

Shaw spoke slowly. "What you doing over here?"

Figuero shrugged his square shoulders. "I don't know. This is where they send me," he answered innocently.

The usually sleepy-eyed sergeant looked on with fully opened eyes, his ears obviously attuned to the conversation.

Shaw continued. "You a US or RA?" Draftees had a US prefix on their serial numbers.

"US."

"You mean you got drafted and you live in Puerto Rico?" Shaw turned to the sergeant. "That's not a state now, is it?"

"Not that I know of."

"We're a territory of the United States," added Figuero. "Laws say we can be drafted."

It was an education for Shaw, but it was difficult for him to accept the fact his country would draft non-Americans and send them to fight in a country they didn't live in.

"Sergeant Kennedy's all situated," Blake was saying two days later. He stood inside the tent at the CAC compound with McHale, Shaw and Figuero. "But you all got orders for Tiger Mountain. They want you there tomorrow. They've been getting a lot of Viet Cong activity at night." He turned to leave, then looked back. "Be extra careful. I don't want any casualties."

CHAPTER 8
Tiger Mountain

This is it, Shaw thought breathlessly. His eyes had just crept downward from the peak of a majestic mountain. Now at the base of the mountain he eyed the dirt road. The jeep he was in had just begun to follow its spiraling path.

The jeep, carrying three men and towing a trailer, strained upward. At several points the driver, McHale, downshifted to second. Quarter of the way up the mountain the road leveled off, revealing a company size compound with tents. Much farther in the distance the hugh American destroyer in the Gulf of Tonkin looked as small as a canoe. McHale hollored at the Marine standing forty yards in the distance. "Where's headquarters?"

The Marine squinted, then stepped forward. At the jeep he said, "Aw, y'all Army. Next level up for headquarters company."

McHale followed the narrow, two lane road upward, slowing down, moving far right and beeping his horn at each blind bend. A third of the way up the mountain the road leveled off again. Barracks replaced tents. McHale drove past two barracks, looking for signs. At the next barrack he saw the words orderly room painted over the door.

Leaving the orderly room, McHale gradually released

his hold on the door until it eased shut; it had slammed shut behind him minutes before. He stepped down and approached the jeep. It was parked close by. Then he spoke to his two men. "We can go down and set up camp. We'll be working with the infantry company." Shaw was in the front, and Figuero was in the back.

Once at the sight, Shaw instructed the other two men on staking the tent. Since they didn't know how, it made him feel like the NCO in charge. And it was almost dark.

Sitting in the tent when darkness descended, Shaw knew they could never have erected it that day without him.

That night, at 2300, static preceded a call on the radio pack which sat in the front seat of the searchlight jeep. "Alpha Sierra, come in, this is Indigo Tango Five."

Sergeant McHale hurried to the front of the vehicle to answer the call. "Indigo Tango Five, this is Alpha Sierra. Go 'head."

"We need some lum on the other side of the road from you. About one hundred twenty-five yards to your left. Over."

"Roger."

"Out."

The sergeant quickly started the engine and then dashed to the rear. He grabbed the handle on the side of the searchlight.

"Hold it!" exclaimed Shaw. "What are you going to do?"

"Get that beam where he wants it!"

"Before you turn it on, let's back the jeep up another fifty yards."

"That 'll give us a wider beam, won't it?" said the sergeant. Then he had Figuero back up the jeep. The sergeant and Shaw sat in the rear.

Half a minute later infantry team #5 squawked softly over the radio. "Alpha Sierra, hurry up with that damn lum! We got movement on the other side of the road."

The sergeant moved the searchlight down toward the road and flicked the switch. The brilliant beam lit everything in its path.

Shaw heard the whiff of rounds passing over his head. "Hit the ground!" he yelled, diving.

A split second later came the sounds of the AK-47 assault rifle. *Pow! Pow! Pow! Pow!*

Rat-tat-tat . . . tat, went infantry team #5's M-60 machine gun.

In a moment there was silence, but only for a moment. "Alpha Sierra! This is Indigo Tango, come in!"

Shaw reached and flicked the searchlight off while McHale rushed to the front and grabbed the transmitt mechanism. "Indigo Tango Five, this is Alpha Sierra. Over," he said, breathing heavily.

"Is everything okay?"

McHale looked in the seats, his hands not pressing the transmitt bar. "Roberto!" he called excitedly.

"I am here, on the ground," Figuero said in a whisper.

McHale bent over the seat, looking to see if his man had been hit.

"I am all right," said Figuero.

McHale let out a deep sigh and pressed the transmitt bar on the hand held mechanism. He said, "Roger, Indigo Tango."

"That illumination was great. We'll get a body count in the morning and credit your team with half the kills. Out."

Shaw stood up. Using his hand as a brush, he removed the dirt and dust from his pants. In a harsh tone of voice he said, "Sarge, I don't dig this shit, using the searchlight as bait. For one thing we're too close. We need to get elevated and shine down on the other side of the road. Tomorrow let's dig out a flat place about a thousand feet up."

"Sounds good," said McHale. "But how in heavens name are we going to get it up there?"

"Chopper, sarge—all the way."

The jeep with its searchlight facing the valley and its front toward the mountain sat anchored by 2 by 4s. The blocks locked all four wheels. The 10 by 12 foot area the crew had cleared out banked toward the valley. Shaw had engineered it that way so the searchlight beam could be angled down to the road. A Marine Chinook had flown eighteen miles from Da Nang to lift, fly and then lower the jeep into its semi-permanent position.

It was night now, and it had come quickly for the crew because they had worked steadily through the day.

But night passed slowly as they fought the urge to sleep. Fortunately the night progressed peacefully. It gave way to an orange sunrise at 0580. At that time the three men, on foot, made their way up the trail they had cut, then to their tent and immediately to their racks.

The village in Tiger Valley was tucked at the base of the hills opposite the 4,100 foot mountain. Military reports claimed the villagers sympathized with and also abetted the Viet Cong. Caches of arms and ammunition had once been confiscated from the tunnels in the hills. Also, large rice harvests always seemed to dwindle all too rapidly for a village of twenty-two families. And on days VC mines were tripped or detected, the early rising villagers had been known to avoid the road like it was a contagious disease.

However, the intelligence reports didn't seem to deter the scores of Marines who visited the skivvey house daily. But, of course, they always carried their weapons.

McHale, Shaw and Figuero weren't deterred either. After dinner they had walked down to the ville. McHale and Figuero went to the skivvey house. It was at one end of the ville and easily spotted as one or two military men left or entered the house every two or three minutes. Shaw went the other way. He wanted to see if there was more to the ville than the skivvey house.

Walking past the hootches, Shaw saw a couple of Marine captains snapping pictures of a pagoda that stood isolated at the end of the village. He stopped briefly, admiring the two-story, ceramic-like structure. It was partly white and mostly pink.

Shaw continued to walk, and he heard music. *A*

string instrument played in a Japanese five tone scale. A folk song of happiness.

Shaw looked ahead, where the music came from. He saw a family of people in front of a hootch. A middle-aged man played the strange instrument that resembled a ukulele, but it only had one string. Shaw lengthened his strides. A moment later he stood in front of the hootch, watching and listening to the man play.

The instrument and music kept Shaw's attention for thirty minutes. Already he had memorized a couple of songs. If a piano was on hand, he could have played them and improvised on the weird chord changes. Then he thought maybe he could learn the strange, exotic-toned instrument. He had studied the fingering of the musician.

The three young ones of the family dispersed with a joyful dance as they went nearby to play. Of the family only the man and woman remained, and she was sitting next to him.

Shaw spoke. "You speak English?"

The man looked puzzled as he stared at Shaw, but the woman said, "I speak. You have question?"

Her dark-brown teeth were unsightly to Shaw, yet he smiled and said, "Can he show me how to play that?" He pointed to the instrument.

The woman turned and spoke Vietnamese to the man, then he spoke the same language to her.

Motioning Shaw over, the woman said, "My husband asks do you play American guitar?" Her manner was friendly.

"Yes," he answered, stretching the truth; he played

around with a friend's guitar for a few months. However, it was five years ago.

After the woman spoke to the man again, the man handed the instrument to Shaw.

The woman added, "Practice it to find the notes."

Shaw lifted the slender-bodied, wooden instrument and held it like the man had, like a guitar. Pressing the gut string with the forefinger of his left hand, he strummed the string with the thumb of his right hand. Then he slid the finger all the way down the narrow fingerboard. He learned the notes were a finger apart and the instrument had a range of two octaves. After ten minutes of dabbling on the instrument, he played a simple jazz tune. He knew jazz was the musical art form that transcended all international boundaries and assembled people of all different cultures and races, as at the international jazz festivals. Jazz, he knew too, was America's only true art contribution to the world. And it was what he loved and played best.

The man and woman listened and looked with interest. For the duration of the tune their eyes never diverted from the source of the music.

When Shaw finished, the man and woman stood and bowed, wide grins on both of their faces.

"Your name?" the woman asked, her dark-brown eyes on Shaw.

"Shaw." He figured it was simpler for them to say than Jimmy.

The man and woman faced each other and said a few words.

Their language required a quick tongue, Shaw noted.

The woman's eyes returned to Shaw. "Shaw, my husband say you #1. You play good music. He say you come back more beaucoup times and play."

Delighted, he responded, "I'll come back everyday I can!"

The Vietnamese woman interpreted for her husband, and their faces simply glowed.

Several nights and days passed, and the evenings found Shaw in the village. He would play jazz, listen to Vietnamese music and drink boiling hot tea at the hootch of the man and woman. His visits were usually no more than forty-five minutes. The nights found Shaw on alert. Nearly every night there had been minor skirmishes between Marines and Viet Cong somewhere along the road. It was believed the VC tried to move goods from the village at night.

The month was June, and one 90° evening Shaw was in the ville. He sat in front of the musician's home. It was later than usual. The setting sun, almost near the horizon, cast a red hue in the western sky. The new moon stood invisible in the blue eastern sky, where a few bright stars twinkled to the bare eye.

"You stay tonight," indicated the woman, looking at Shaw. "I go and have mama-son send you a pretty girl."

Surprised, Shaw stared at the woman under his dark glasses, trying to figure out from her facial expression why she felt he needed a girl. It had never been brought up before. She was straight faced, however. "I can't stay," he responded. "I have guard duty tonight."

SHAW'S NAM 157

The woman said something to the man and then stepped into the hootch.

The man started playing an eerie sounding melody on his instrument, like those in a movie soundtrack where the hero is about to step into an ominous situation. The tempo was as slow as a sad blues.

The woman returned to the front with a kettle, like always. She poured boiling hot tea into clay made cups setting on the table.

And Shaw, as usual, pulled his cup of green tea to the edge and then dipped sugar cane into it. After a moment he stirred the tea with the cane. Then he sipped the sweetened beverage.

Half a minute later he began to realize what the music meant—death, as no one else had drank tea. He tried to keep his eyes open as he reached feebly at the woman with a half clenched fist, knowing he had been poisoned. But why, he thought, looking at the woman with nearly closed eyes. Then he slumped in the chair, fully unconscious.

0525, Shaw groggily came around, immediately realizing that he had only been drugged. He rose stiffly from the straw mat he had been lying on. He bent down and lifted his rifle. Although he didn't see anyone, he knew that he was in the front room of the man and woman's hootch. He lifted the wooden strut that held the front door secure. He pushed the door open and went outside. The wee light of dawn limited his vision to just the ville. It seemed deserted. The doors and windows of the hootches were all shut, and nobody stirred around the ville. With their chirps, howls and screaks, only birds, animals and insects communicated.

Shaw began walking toward the road that spiraled up Tiger Mountain, wondering if he would get an article 15 for being AWOL from duty. Then, on the road running between the village and mountain, he saw Viet Cong laid wasted on the ground. With the blood circulation in his body now running rapidly, he looked further down the road and saw more bodies. A platoon of dead VC, he estimated. He quickened his steps, and shortly he was running. Up the spiraling road he went. In three minutes he covered half a mile of bends and straightaways, being challenged strongly at two guard posts.

"What happened!" Shaw said, opening the flap to his tent and stepping inside.

"Shaw! Shaw!" McHale said in disbelief, opening his eyes and jumping from his rack like he saw a ghost. "Figuero and I thought you got captured or killed in the ville with those other Marines."

Figuero was sound asleep on his cot, his head under the thin poncho liner.

"What other Marines?" Shaw asked, speaking much faster than usual.

"The VC cut the throats of two Marines in the whore house last night. A squad went out last night looking for the missing Marines and you. When they only found the dead Marines, I figured you had gotten captured!"

"What about all those dead VC?" A disgusted frown was on his face.

"Where the hell you been? Those dumb bastards, a whole company of 'em, tried to overrun this base.

Didn't you hear all the noise—recoiless rifles, mortars, machine guns, flares, evacuation helicopters?"

"Not really," answered Shaw. He wasn't speaking as fast as a moment ago. He reflected on the actions and thoughts of the man and woman. They're beautiful, he thought. Then he continued. "I got knocked-out in the ville."

"The ville! Captain Walls lost sixteen men. He was mad as hell. He started to have the ville blown away with artillery fire. He thinks the whole village is nothing but VC."

"He's wrong! A family of villagers saved me! I'll tell him. I know some of the villagers, and I think they just help the VC because they're at their mercy."

"Maybe you should tell the captain. But first you tell me what all happened. I got to make a report. Higher-ups know you were missing."

Shaw told his story to McHale, and later that morning, after some sleep, he told it to the Marine company commander. And he tried to convince him that the villagers weren't VC.

The captain, who was stubborn and unconscionable, told Shaw that if he could have had his way, he would have blown the ville—people and all—away months ago. But the captain admitted his superior wouldn't let him.

"So you (are) Shaw?" asked Lance Corporal Radford Johnson in a cool manner. He was the bootleg barber for Charlie company. Johnson, who was black, cut white Marines' hair, too. This was a rarity because whites, like blacks, had a hangup about the opposite race cutting their hair. They figured the guy just couldn't do it right since it wasn't like theirs.

Johnson ran the electric clippers across the top of Shaw's head. A ball of woolly, black hair fell lightly to the pallet. The pallet elevated the wooden chair Shaw sat on inside the tent Johnson shared with three other Marines. It was evening, and the other three were out playing basketball.

"Yeah, that's me." Shaw said coolly in return.

"I've been hearing how you fought off those VC in the ville last night."

Shaw smiled. "Is that what they're saying? What makes 'em say that?"

"You made it back after being down there all night, didn't ya?"

"Yeah," said Shaw, deciding not to dispel the rumor. "Bad experience. I don't want to talk about it anymore."

"Yeah, I can dig that." Johnson sipped from a sweaty can of beer, then returned, "This cut's on me. You a bad dude."

Several days passed, and Shaw hadn't returned to the village since the night the VC attacked the compound. He hadn't because he didn't know how to face the musician and his wife. Did they expect him to be happy or angry, he wondered, knowing how peculiar their philosophy was. He remembered the time when the woman told him that she and her husband had no fear of dying. He could only assume it was because they had flirted with death everyday of their lives. The woman had added that her people had been at war ever since she could remember.

Shaw wanted to thank them for protecting him, but he finally decided not to visit them again.

He never really understood why himself.

Perched high in the sky, the chameleon-like sun was now yellow. It gave off intense rays that heated the air around the lower third of Tiger Mountain to 90°.

Platoon Sergeant Blake visited his men at Tiger Mountain for the first time at the location. Standing inside his men's tent, he spoke to McHale. "How things been going here lately? I've been getting your reports. Seems like this was a hot place for awhile."

Shaw twisted in his rack when he heard Blake's voice. He opened his eyes, blurily focusing them on the platoon sergeant. "You got any letters for me, Sergeant Blake?"

"You know I have," said Blake, grinning and turning toward Shaw. "I got three. If you didn't get so much mail, I wouldn't have to make so many trips."

"I haven't seen you in a month," said Shaw, still lying in the rack.

McHale finally took the chance to answer his superior. "Everything's been calm since the Marines wiped out those VC ten days ago."

"Well," returned Blake, "I guess that's why the Marines want you guys at another location. They got some kind of operation going on northwest of here. They want a minimum number of support troops, so I'm going to leave you with Shaw, the most experienced man."

"Good," said McHale without hesitating.

Blake spoke. "Wake Figuero up, Mac, and get him to pack. I'll take him back to base camp with me today. You guys 'll be moving out tomorrow. The Marines will provide you with everything during the operation."

Shaw was bitter and took it out on the Marines. "Have they got anything?" He pulled on his trousers. "They ought to give somebody at least a two day notice." Although he said nothing about it, he was actually upset that he didn't get to go to base camp. It only seemed fair, he thought, that the men should be rotated.

"Only consolation I have," said Blake, facing Shaw, "is that you guys won't have to work tonight—my orders."

Big fuckin deal.

CHAPTER 9
LZ Baker

Landing Zone Baker was one of those small bases nobody particularly wanted to be assigned to. Located near the Laotian border, it was isolated from any large U.S. military complex. Da Nang was the closest at 30 miles southeast. The only direct way to LZ Baker was by helicopter. No roads and bridges had yet been constructed that cut all the way to the LZ—across valleys and rivers, over hills, and through jungles—from Route 1. The native inhabitants were the Montagnard tribesmen. And, although they were allies, they were not as congenial as the regular Vietnamese.

On a large hill that looked like its top had been sliced off, Baker was situated on the flat clearing. Ninety-five feet below the hill a jungle of tropical trees rose and surrounded the LZ for miles. Four trails, wide enough for 2½ ton trucks, twisted through the jungle below, and one ran up to Baker. Far west of the LZ, four miles at the closest point, a mountain range extended North and South.

Helicopters landed at Baker to bring in supplies for the Marine battalion which was scattered around the LZ. Baker was constructed because of operation Python, an operation initiated to choke North Vietnamese resupply. This supply line, the clandestine Ho Chi Minh Trail, was believed to run down South Vietnam near the Laotian and Cambodian borders.

It was 0960 when McHale backed the jeep and trailer out of the Marine Chinook at Baker. The base was the size of a minor league baseball park. Tents and bunkers absorbed more than half of the space. A landing pad took up the remainder. McHale drove from under the turbulence of the helicopter blades and stopped, where a few seconds later Shaw jumped in the passenger seat. McHale proceeded forward, looking at the mountains to the west. "This is a nice view."

Shaw turned his head and eyed McHale. "Yeah. Only thing—hills and mountains bring trouble. That's been my experience over here."

"You're right. Like the one we just left. But pretty scenery it was, the ocean and all."

"The whole country's beautiful," Shaw emphasized. "It would be a nice place to vacation if things were modern and this war wasn't going on. Just think if you could stay in a lodge on the side of Tiger Mountain, up there in the clouds."

"It would be fantastic."

"Yeah."

After McHale got instructions from the officer in charge of the compound, he and Shaw pitched their tent at the designated location.

As McHale and Shaw rested inside the tent, McHale spoke, lying on his cot. "That first lieutenant wants us to use the searchlight as a beacon, to bring in choppers after dark, and use it as a reference point for other aircraft, like gunships. You ever done that?"

"Not really," returned Shaw, sitting on his cot. "But it sounds easy, and it's a change."

"I agree. And one other thing: have you ever built a bunker? The lieutenant says we need one."

"All we need to do is dig two foxholes and place a quarter section of galvanized culvert over each one. Then we can lay sandbags over the culverts."

"We'll do it after lunch then. And I better tell you right now that lunch is the only hot meal of the day. They fly it in here, and sometimes it doesn't come 'cause the choppers got other priorities."

"Shit. We got to stay healthy. What other priority beats that?"

"Missing two or three hot meals a week won't hurt, Jimmy. Look at the guys out in the bush. They miss hot meals and hours of sleep every single day."

"Yeah, I've seen 'em, and they look bad, too."

"It's a good thing you're in artillery instead of the infantry," added McHale, smiling.

"Yeah, don't I know it," Shaw countered coolly.

Complete darkness had just set in. The time was 2140. McHale and Shaw had been working since dusk and were scheduled to do so until midnight.

The searchlight jeep, with the two soldiers inside, sat on the edge of the landing pad. Twenty-five feet away was a guard bunker. Three other guard bunkers encircled the LZ, and concertina barbed wire poked around the perimeter. Nearly 100 foot of flat ground bordered the wire before the ground sloped steeply to the jungle below.

Seated in the front of the jeep with Shaw, McHale said, "There's supposed to be some heavy equipment lifted in tonight. They're doing it at night so NVA reconnaissance won't spot it right away."

A split-second after McHale had spoken, static buzzed over the radio pack sitting on the dashboard. Then came communication. "Alpha Sierra, this is Charlie Papa. Do you read me? Over?"

McHale grabbed the transmitter mike, pushed in the lever and said, "Charlie Papa, this is Alpha Sierra. I read you loud and clear. How do you read me? Over?"

"I read you the same. We have a hotel approaching from the east, approximately five minutes away. It requests your lima at 60° from the ground. Over."

"Will do immediately, Charlie Papa. Over."

"Roger and out."

As McHale started the jeep, Shaw rushed to the rear and aimed the searchlight to the east and virtually straight up. Gradually he brought it down 30°. He flipped the switch, and a beam of light penetrated thousands of feet into a sky that was without a layer of clouds.

A minute later the fluttering sound of a helicopter echoed through the night air.

Two-and-a-half minutes later the Army searchlight team was instructed by the command post to extinguish the light.

Instantly, they did.

In the next thirty seconds the long Sikorsky Crane helicopter lowered the first of a half battery of 105mm howitzers. In a net the cannon hung from the craft on a thick rope cable. Without a fuselage, the Sikorsky resembled a flying praying mantis, and its floodlamp eyeballs placed the necessary lighting on the landing pad. Once the heavy net containing the howitzer and crates of ammunition touched the ground, a Marine rushed out and unhooked the net from the cable. The Marine then ran off the landing pad. The giant helicopter, its length, slightly greater than that of a Grayhound bus, propelled itself straight up, creating a cloud of dust. Then the craft flew southeast. Within ten minutes two other crane helicopters made identical dumps.

Six men, two to a net, removed the cannons and ammunition. They then hitched the cannons to the rear of the deuce-and-a-half trucks and loaded the ammunition onto the beds.

On their two wheels, the cannons were towed to the tent area.

With the Army jeep still at the edge of the landing pad, Shaw said, "Wasn't nothing to that, sarge. I wonder how many more copters we'll have to bring in tonight?"

"That should be it."

"Do you think those cannons will stay here?"

"They will, according to that first lieutenant. And he thinks that's unfortunate."

"Why's that?"

"Because they're supposed to be used in a crossfire. He doesn't think they should be used on this LZ; they might provoke an attack. Can you blame him? There's not that many men here."

"There's some pros and cons," said Shaw, his blase' voice indicating he wasn't really concerned about the issue.

It was now 2385. Looking toward the Laotian border, beyond the horizon, Shaw noticed what he thought was lightning. "It looks like a storm might be coming our way tonight," he said as he stood near a Marine PFC on guard duty outside the bunker.

The helmeted Marine with his M-16 in hand added with a grin, "Charlie probably wished it was only a storm. Those are clusters of bombs from a B-52." The Marine eyed the western sky and said, "Listen."

Shaw became still, then after a moment he said, "I don't hear anything but the sound of animals and insects."

"Do you see anything?" The stars hardly twinkled; the sky was that clear.

Shaw tilted his head and then answered, "Naw."

"That's why Charlie fears the shit out of those B-52s," the Marine commented, leveling his head.

"Yeah. I see what you mean," said Shaw, bringing his head and eyes down. "Well, I better step back to my jeep. I know my sergeant's about ready to leave."

"Okay."

"See you around."

Boom! Boom! Boom!   Boom! Boom! Boom!..., the 105s voiced the next morning.

Being awakened by the repetitiveness of the cannons, Shaw rose to dress. All he needed to do was slip on his boots, shirt and glasses. In the field he always slept in his pants and underwear. He wanted to be mostly dressed if there was an attack.

After Shaw dressed, he glanced at the watch on the sleeping sergeant's wrist, then stepped outside the tent. The time was 10 o'clock. Shaw walked toward the half battery of cannons as they continued to fire. As he got close, the cannons sounded extremely loud.

But in between firings he could hear the Marine corporal tell his six men—two to a gun—when and where to fire. Since the corporal had a phone to his ear, Shaw figured information was coming from the FDC bunker. He guessed fire direction was getting its information over radio from a forward observer.

During a pause in firings Shaw inquired, "What kind of round you using, corporal?"

"HE with a delay," returned the brawny-armed corporal. His shirt sleeves were rolled to his elbows. He kept his eyes on the minor elevation adjustments his men made on the howitzers. Painted in white on the steel barrel of one howitzer was the name Heartbreaker. Another howitzer was Eve of Destruction. The third was Rip-off.

Seeing the elevation of the cannons at more than 45° and knowing the round wouldn't go right off on contact, Shaw knew the 33 pound high explosive would dig itself into the ground or a bunker before it exploded.

The cannons shot another series of rounds and then the corporal spoke happily. "That's it! We got some hits."

"How many bunkers did you blow?" asked Shaw.

The corporal, in a sweat-soiled fatigue cap, looked at Shaw seemingly surprised; his blue-gray eyes had widened. "We blew four NVA bunkers, but I don't know how many kills we got. The FO said the platoon ran like hell down the hill when the first bunker blew. The gooks are close, man—three miles."

Beads of sweat popped on Shaw's forehead. Even though it was hot—96 on a cloudy day, it wasn't the heat that made him sweat. He had become acclimated to it and didn't perspire from it ordinarily. His sweaty reaction attested to how he felt about the NVA being so close. "And how close do those FOs get?"

"I'd say about a mile. They've got good field glasses. But then again, since they're recon guys, they might even get closer. They think they're the baddest son-of-bitches in the Marines," the corporal said, a sound of resentment in his voice. "They got a kill ratio of 100 to 1."

Shaw's eyebrows raised. "Yeah? I'd like to meet 'em."

"No telling when they'll be back. They can live off the land." Then he pointed to a bunker. It was detached from the regular area. "They stay there. But don't let them catch you meddling in their bunker."

"Ain't no need for me to go in there if they're not there."

"What's your full name, Shaw?"

"Jimmy Shaw. Indianapolis. And yours?"

"Harry Carter. I'm from a little city in Penn called Camp Hill. If I see those guys, I'll look you up. I know where you guys park that searchlight jeep."

"Okay, I'll talk to you later.

That night McHale and Shaw brought two Chinooks in. Other than that the night basically went the same as the one before.

The next day at 1150 Corporal Harry Carter stepped into the Army tent. Carter, of average height and sturdy build, looked his age, 21. His deeply tanned face was cleanly shaved all over, and the hair around his sweat-soiled cap was reddish. Carter spoke as he saw Shaw sitting on his cot, writing a letter. "Those recon guys got back last night. I told them an Army PFC was interested in the way they spotted."

Shaw lifted his head, eyed Carter and said, "Okay. Thanks."

Sergeant McHale closed the James Bond novel he had been reading, then looked at Shaw.

Observing McHale, Shaw spoke. "Sarge, this is Corporal Carter." Shaw's eyes shifted to Carter, then back to McHale. "He's in charge of those noisy cannons." A smirk was on Shaw's face.

The sergeant rose and extended his hand; the corporal stepped forward and extended his, and they shook.

"Glad to have you here," said Carter. "Things are looking up. I was here two days waiting on my guns. Since then you guys and a mortar crew have come in."

"How long do you think this operation will last?" asked the sergeant.

"I wish I knew. But if it lasts until October, that'll be fine with me. My thirteen month tour will be up then. I like it better in the bush. Nobody fucks with you. Back in Da Nang is too much like the States. Inspections, reveile and that kind of petty shit."

The corporal turned and looked at Shaw. "If you got a minute, I'll introduce you to those recon guys."

"Yeah, yeah," said Shaw enthusiastically. "Let's go."

As they stepped out of the tent, Carter asked Shaw, "How long you been in the Nam?"

"Not long. About three or four months. I don't even keep up with it like I used to."

"You haven't been on R&R then?"

R&R was a three day rest and recuperation period in some exotic city as close as Bangkok, Thailand or as far as Sydney, Australia. The period was given to all American servicemen serving a tour of duty in Vietnam. Only transportation was free, however.

"Naw. I'll wait 'til I've done at least half my time. That way the rest of it will seem down hill. You been?"

"Oh yeah. Singapore. Fast city. And lots of broads: pretty ones, brown ones, white ones, yellow ones. Check it out!"

"I just might. It sounds like my kind of place."

It only took them a minute to reach the recon bunker.

"Sergeant Stone," yelled Carter before he stepped through the passageway.

"What the fuck you want, Carter?" a deep voice resounded from inside the bunker.

"I got the guy from the Army with me."

"All right, y'all come on in."

Carter and Shaw stepped down and into the bunker. The sunlight coming in through the narrow entrance lit its interior.

Stone was lying on one of the two cots. Boxes marked *Long Range Rations* were under his cot. Stone's size 13 feet extended four inches past the end of his six foot cot. His head was even with the other end. He only wore green briefs. His lean, muscular, dark-brown legs looked like those of a broadjumper. His right leg was flawed by a healed scar that ran across the front of his thigh. Twenty stitches it had once taken. His beard was thick with black hairs. Shaw guessed he had a shaving profile—a medical statement that exempted him from shaving. Unlike most men who wore beards, he wore no mustache. The hair on his head was beady and cut into a short afro.

Stone raised his head and looked at Carter, then Shaw. He clenched his fist, lifted it in the air and said, "What's going on, brother?"

The clenched fist was generally mistaken by some whites as a sign of black power, a radical concept, just as the way some blacks felt about the rebel flag. However, even though blacks called the clenched fist the *power* sign, they laid it on each other as a greeting and show of unity.

"Looks like you got it," Shaw replied easily.

"I'm just trying to catch up on some zeeze. Me and my partner didn't get in until two. We couldn't move until midnight. All kind of gook patrols out there."

"Where's he at?" asked Shaw.

"Bear? He supposed to be bringing me some chow back. He's probably down at the mess tent eating like a pig."

Stone shifted his half-closed, brown eyes on Carter and continued, "Y'all did some decent shooting for a change. Next time make sure they load a willy peeter round for the spotter. And when I say 50 yards to the right, don't go 80."

"You can get on FDC's ass for that," Carter said in a raised voice.

"I sure in the fuck will!" said Stone, his eyes now wide open. "Who's in charge down there?"

Just then a heavyset, white Marine squeezed through

the passageway. In his hand was a metal plate stacked with food.

Shaw stared at the Marine, guessing he stood six-one and weighed two-fifteen.

The top half of the Marine's body was covered only with a green v-neck, t-shirt. His shotputter-like arms were covered with straight, brown hair, bulging half an inch. Hair bulged on his chest and around the neckline of his t-shirt, too.

"You gotta be Bear?" said Shaw with a smile.

"Yeah, doggie," Bear answered, facing Shaw. His tone was nasty. "Where'd you come from?"

"He's cool," injected Stone, now sitting up on the cot.

Bear stepped across the small bunker and handed Stone the plate of food.

Stone held the plate in one hand and looked at the food on it. He reached for the food with the other hand and said, "Same o' shit—roast beef and parsley potatoes." He stuck both in his mouth, chewed it quickly and followed it with some bread.

Shaw spoke. "I just stopped in to see how y'all did forward observing." He looked shyly at Bear. "I used to be in FDC."

"You did?" Bear said; a slight smile had replaced the snarl he had had on his face. "If you're good, those idiots in the FDC bunker could use you. We called 50 right, and they went 100."

"Come on, Bear. It wasn't that bad," mumbled Stone. His mouth was stuffed with the 'same o' shit.' "It was more like 70 yards."

Bear turned toward Carter and finally spoke. "How's it going, Harry?"

"All right, sarge. I hear you guys spotted a lot of NVA?"

"Beaucoup! I'd say your artillery took out eight. We get credit for half, and I got two more with my sniper rifle."

Shaw's eyes moved around the bunker and stopped on a M-14 rifle; a telescopic scope was mounted on top.

Taking his eyes off the rifle and looking at Bear, he spoke. "What's the effective range on your rifle?"

The Marine responded nonchalantly, "Oh, I can hit a gook between the eyes from 1,000 yards."

"Pretty good," returned Shaw.

"Damn good!" insisted Bear.

Although Shaw was beginning to dislike Bear's arrogant attitude, he thought he could relate to Stone. But since Stone was busy eating, he decided to leave. "I'm glad I stopped by and met you dudes. Probably check y'all out later."

"Yeah," mumbled Stone.

Having a deep frown on his face, Bear said nothing.

As Shaw stepped out of the bunker, Carter followed. Ten yards away from the bunker Shaw turned to Carter and demanded, "What's wrong with that dude, Bear? He don't like brothers or something?"

"He's just a mean son-of-a-bitch. Two mandatory tours in the Nam, you don't expect him to be nice. And they put him in recon because he's been hit twice. Usually that's the way they do infantry corporal and sergeants."

"And Stone?"

"First tour. Already got two purple hearts. They

let him wear that beard 'cause the left side of his face is healing from shrapnel wounds.''

"Anyway," Shaw said, reaching out his hand and then shaking Carter's, "thanks for turning me on to 'em, but I'm not all that enthused about checking 'em out again."

They released hands and Carter commented, "They just think they're hot shit 'cause they're recon."

It was 2275 and the fifth night McHale and Shaw had been at LZ Baker. Earlier in the evening the searchlight crew had performed the duties it had been brought in to do. But now that several firefights had erupted within three miles of Baker, the LZ was on a watch. The searchlight crew was now on duty to scan the perimeter, to spot enemy soldiers or deter them with the bright light.

Shaw had stopped taking tranquilizers weeks ago. His nerves were steady, but at Baker he had felt menaced by the close presence of the NVA ever since the second day. It had caused him to take rifle practice daily, shooting at the snakes in the jungle below the LZ. The fourth day he had shot off the head of a darting blue racer from a distance of 150 feet. He felt then he was the marksman he wanted to be.

But now the searchlight jeep was idling fifteen yards from one of the guard bunkers. McHale and Shaw scanned on infrared. If there were any enemy soldiers nearby, they wanted to eliminate them, not deter them to strike some other time. But, as they scanned, they spotted no enemy.

Shaw laid the special binoculars in the rear of the jeep and turned toward the nearby bunker. He saw a Marine lance corporal sitting on top of the sandbagged bunker, puffing a cigarette. It was no ordinary cigarette, Shaw gathered by the smell. Vietnamese hashish, he remembered; he had sampled some at Con Lo.

With a firefight raging two-and-a-half miles to the west, Shaw knew it was no time to be getting high. As he stood at the side of the jeep, he could plainly see the muzzle fire and red tracers of the small arms used in the firefight. The sounds of those arms were faintly audible. And every now and then a white flare lit the sky.

It perturbed Shaw the more he thought about it: the Marine risking the lives of the men at the base because his head was bad. "Hey, man," Shaw yelled, getting the attention of the Marine on top of the bunker. "How you gonna keep a clear head smoking that herb?"

"Don't worry about it," returned the Marine not speaking loudly, his eyes staying on the stars above.

A bitter look darkened Shaw's face. He wanted to chastise the Marine lance corporal.

From the rear of the jeep McHale quinted at Shaw and then quickly stepped to the side of it. He spoke quietly "It's not worth arguing about. We're here. We'll be on guard all night, and there's another Marine resting inside the . . ."

WOOM! A B-40 straight line rocket suddenly exploded on the bunker.

McHale and Shaw jumped like toads. Then they dove for the ground. Shaw held onto his rifle.

Keeping his eyes open, Shaw saw the Marine lance

corporal rising in the air six feet and the bunker caving-in.

Ca-Boom! went another explosion. It was a satchel charge at the concertina barbed wire. Shaw knew the first line of enemy would be sappers. Their specialty was explosives. Their targets were usually ammunition dumps, fuel depots, and barbed wire perimeters.

Things happened rapidly around Shaw. Two of the land mines in front of the barbed wire went off; he saw the limbs and disfigured bodies of NVA soldiers fly into the air. He heard McHale say *retreat*. Then he saw five green uniformed enemy rush through the blown opening. He was composed enough to flip his M-16 to automatic, point and then fire. He hit the first two; they stumbled forward several feet, then fell. He stopped firing his weapon, realizing he had killed for the first time.

But he felt neither compassion nor regret; he knew it was them or him.

The hard hitting M-60 at the next closest guard bunker opened up. *Rat-tat-tat-tat-tat*. It knocked down the other three NVA in their tracks.

Then, on his belly, Shaw crawled. It was almost like he was one of the snakes he had shot as a target; he crawled swiftly away from enemy gunfire. He moved toward the tent and bunker area, not knowing NVA were pouring through the opening. He paid no attention to the daylight illumination of a flare, the rattle of machine gun fire, the whiff of bullets, the whistle of mortar rounds, the boom of explosions, or the screams of men in pain and fear.

Near a foxhole-bunker, Shaw stood to run the last fifteen feet.

"Get down!" a familiar voice cried to his flank.

Shaw dived, head first, into the bunker. Then he heard the pop of a M-79 grenade launcher. A second-and-a-half later the grenade exploded. Shaw quickly sat up and looked out the bunker. Fifty feet out front he saw the smoke clearing from the explosion. A second later he saw four NVA sprawled on the ground. He then turned to what had been his flank and saw Bear behind a shallow wall of sandbags, loading a 40mm round into the grenade launcher. The launcher was broken down like a shotgun.

Shaw extracted the nearly empty magazine from his rifle and inserted a full one. He put the weapon in semi-automatic and took aim. He began picking off the approaching enemy like they were targets in a shooting gallery. Four fell from the rounds of his rifle.

Countless more fell from other fire.

Several marines had fallen also. Most were helpless as enemy mortar rounds fell and exploded inside their foxholes.

A lull came in the battle, an undeclared cease fire. No weapons fired. No enemy was visible as flares shot upward.

A minute elapsed. Then suddenly, NVA, most stoned crazy off cocaine, began rushing forth in a wave, two squads.

Machine gun and rifle fire erupted throughout Baker again.

Eight seconds later a new wave came. Under a cover of their exploding mortars, they threw satchel charges that had two and three times the kick of hand grenades. They also fired rifles and machine guns like the first wave. Their advance was deep. Another fifty yards and bayonets could have replaced bullets.

Suddenly Shaw heard the familiar boom of a 105 and saw the bright orange muzzle flash out of the corner of his eye.

Enemy then screamed at the top of their voices, fell and quivered like aerosoled mosquitoes.

Shaw turned toward the 105s. Two were overturned, but Carter had lowered the barrel on the undamaged one. The barrel was at ground level, and Carter was in back of it, reloading. No doubt a beehive round, Shaw thought. The round was like a giant shotgun shell, only it expelled thousands of sharp, pin-like, metal pieces instead of a hundred or so blunt buckshots. Looking at the punctured faces of the fallen enemy, it was easy to see why the round was called a beehive.

Several seconds later another wave of NVA rushed. They, too, fired AK-47s and threw satchel charges, until Carter pulled the lantern cord on Heartbreaker. *Boooom!* The smell of burnt gunpowder quickly saturated the air.

A dozen sharp cries of agony pierced the night.

Finally, M-60 machine gun fire and M-16 rifle fire ended the NVA's unsuccessful attempt to eliminate LZ Baker. Yet, the enemy succeeded in destroying two 105mm howitzers, a searchlight, 4 bunkers, 6 tents, 46 of their own, and 13 American lives.

Fighting men never sleep during a full-blown battle, nor do they sleep for hours and sometimes not soundly for days afterward. It takes hours just to tend to the wounded and evacuate them, along with the dead. Then it takes just as long, or even days, for some to overcome the trauma of battle—friends being killed next to them, themselves killing and almost being killed. And for a few, it takes a lifetime.

It was early morning before Shaw and McHale fell asleep. They had helped tidy the constantly illuminated camp. Dead NVA had been thrown into the back of a deuce-and-a-half. Downed and ripped tents had been completely removed.

It was early morning also when McHale had radioed base camp on the master transmitter-receiver in the FDC bunker. He had told an Army spec 4 to inform Blake of the destroyed searchlight.

The specialist had told McHale that the message would be relayed to Platoon Sergeant Blake after breakfast and a reply sent back before noon.

It was 1150 when a Marine courier handed Sergeant McHale a sealed envelope. Sitting on his cot, McHale politely took the letter, thanked the departing courier, and then hastily tore open the letter. The contents read:

Sergeant McHale,

Please be advised that no searchlights are available. As a result you and PFC Shaw will report to platoon base camp in Da Nang. Return on a resupply helicopter as soon as possible. The commander at Landing Zone Baker has been informed of the situation.

Dated: 7/3/68
Time: 1140
Signed: 1st Lt. Green

After reading the message, McHale folded the piece of paper and stuck it in his upper shirt pocket. A Texas smile was on his tired face, which beneath his eyes was puffy. He turned his head toward Shaw and spoke jubilantly. "We're getting out a here!"

"Yeah! When?"

"ASAP!"

"You're bullshiting?" questioned Shaw, lying tense, waiting for reaffirmation.

"The Army can't spare any more searchlights for Marine operations."

"All right," exclaimed Shaw, sitting up. "I'm sure glad the Army don't have a lot of everything." He jumped to his feet. "I'm going down and holler at Carter, then see Stone and Bear. I got to thank Bear. If it wasn't for him, I might not be here."

Shaw found all three men inside the mess tent eating lunch. The three proved to be buoyant; they joked and laughed with Shaw about how much he would miss the excitement at the LZ.

CHAPTER 10
Da Nang

Upon seeing hundreds of military barracks, each seemingly freshly painted, and hundreds of strolling American servicemen, who wore caps rather than helmets, Shaw felt a sense of security. He was in Da Nang now, sitting in the rear of Sergeant Blake's three-quarter ton truck. Blake was driving back to platoon base camp at Freedom Hill which was in a remote area of Da Nang. Twenty minutes ago Blake had picked up Shaw and McHale from the helicopter pad at Red Beach.

The drive lasted forty minutes.

Now in front of the orderly room, Blake parked his truck.

Shaw rose from the bench seat, moved toward the tailgate and leaped over it like a hurdler. Landing erect, he took notice of the U-shaped arrangement of the eight barracks. The orderly room was at one end and the transit barrack opposite.

Shaw lowered the tailgate, pulled his heavy footlocker forward and then lifted it out of the bed of the truck. Then he stepped briskly to the transit barrack.

Quickly returning to the truck to get his other gear, he heard McHale's voice. "Come on, Jimmy. The lieutenant wants to see us." McHale stood at the door of the orderly room.

Shaw left his gear in the truck. A moment later he followed McHale into the platoon leader's office. There, they stopped just in front of the metal desk, and McHale spoke. "Sergeant McHale and PFC Shaw reporting, sir."

Ignoring McHale's statement and keeping the two enlisted men standing at parade rest, First Lieutenant Green leafed through a thick manual. Only the vibrating motor of the window air-conditioner broke the silence. Several seconds later Green slapped closed the manual, raised his head and said, "At ease, men."

McHale and Shaw brought their own feet together and their hands from behind. They folded their hands in front as they stood informal.

"We've got two spankin brand new searchlights coming down from headquarters," began Green, his blue eyes centered on the sergeant. "They'll be down, hopefully, next week. So until then you'll be assigned office duty."

Green moved his head a bit. It was full of black, short-clipped hair. He looked squarely at Shaw. "And you'll be a relief man for different crews." Green shifted his eyes to McHale, then back to Shaw. "I brought you men in to tell you I'm proud of what the Marine commander up North said."

"They said something good, sir?" Shaw inserted promptly.

"Absolutely. He said you guys busted your asses when you had to."

Shaw blushed, and McHale's familiar grin appeared.

The lieutenant spoke again. "My door is usually open if any problems arise. But try to go through the chain of command if it's not a real serious matter.

So if there are no questions, I'll see you men around camp."

Shaw stepped into the PX at Freedom Hill. The PX was half the size of a stateside supermarket. With fluorescent lighting it looked as modern as one, and would have been if it had had central air instead of floor fans. The PX was as full with American servicemen as a department store with people on a Saturday afternoon.

Walking and browsing, Shaw saw American staples and confections. He saw Japanese cameras and hi-fi equipment. Stopping at a glass counter that displayed watches and rings, he checked out the price tags. He quickly realized the prices of the jewelry was just about two-thirds that for the same quality back home. Even though he had been sending most of his money home to be saved and to help his mother, he had enough in his wallet to buy a very good watch. He knew that he needed one, yet the glitter of a diamond ring and its modest price tag kept sparkling in his eye. A third of a carat stone for 200 bills, a bargain and investment, he thought. And going home flashing it on his pinky finger to his partners and lady would be impressive.

"Let me have that rock," said Shaw, pointing to the glittering, white stone. "Can I put fifty dollars down on it for lay-away?"

"Sure," the oriental gentleman—dressed in a white short-sleeve shirt, tan bermuda shorts, and white socks—said. He bent over and unlocked his side of the counter. He removed the ring and handed it to Shaw.

After Shaw inspected the ring and was satisfied that it was genuine, he gave the salesman the money and returned the ring.

"Do you need anything else, Mr. Shaw?" the salesman asked while making out a receipt.

"Yeah, a watch," said Shaw, pointing to the inside of the counter.

Once again the salesman reached inside the counter and pulled out a small, stiff case. "You mean this?"

Shaw had been looking away at the crowd of servicemen. When he turned and saw the watch was a Seiko, he exclaimed, "Naw!" Then he caught himself. Quieter, he continued. "I mean I want the American made Bulova right next to it."

The comfortably dressed salesman pulled out the watch. It was 14 karat gold with a small .1 carat diamond where the numeral 12 would have been. The price tag read $59.95.

Shaw removed his wallet and took out the remaining $85—half his monthly salary now. In Vietnam everybody was paid combat duty pay. It increased Shaw's monthly salary by 25%. But he often had negative thoughts about his salary. A funky $170 a month, he would think, wishing he would have gone airborne to get jump pay, too. He peeled off three twenties and paid for the watch that had won his heart.

Moving away from the counter, Shaw set the time and date on his watch to four-twelve and the third, just as the salesman had told him. It being the first watch he owned, Shaw was careful as he wound it. Now he could keep up with the time and date. And, he knew in eighteen minutes the mess hall would be serving dinner.

It was like Cam Ranh Bay all over again, thought Shaw, standing in a long mess hall line. Nearly thirty soldiers were in front of him. He recalled that at Tiger mountain the chow lines were never allowed to be more than five or six men long. It would have been unexcusable to have more men than that taken out by one enemy mortar round.

"Jimmy Shaw! Jimmy Shaw!"

Recognizing Figuero's voice, Shaw spun to the rear, a wide smile on his face.

Figuero, his teeth gleaming, moved forward quickly. In a few seconds he stopped right in front of Shaw. He reached out his hand, and they shook like soul brothers—the black handshake.

However, Shaw's grip loosened and smile faded as he discovered Figuero outranked him. Personally, he had little against Figuero. But he questioned the system, the qualification factor, wondering how Figuero could be a spec 4 barely being able to pitch a tent, fire the M-16 or understand English. Shaw questioned the seniority factor, too, knowing he had been in the country two months longer than Figuero. Shaw thought about it a second longer and concluded that Figuero had been in base camp kissing ass.

"What's been happening?" asked Shaw through a grin that was a bit narrower than a moment ago.

"Nothing. Nothing much. Where's the sergeant?"

"He's around. Probably hanging out with the NCOs now."

The line moved steadily. The two men moved with it as they talked.

"What you do at the new base?" asked Figuero.

"Kicked ass, man."

Figuero laughed sarcastically. "You mean kiss ass."

"That's funny," returned Shaw. A smirk had replaced his grin. "I thought that's how you got promoted."

"What you say?"

Shaw spoke slowly. "Kissing ass. Ain't that how you got promoted?"

"Bullshit!" snarled Figuero. "I don't kiss nobody's ass. You be like me. Stay squared away here, and you'll get spec 4."

"You're right," said Shaw, a serious look on his face. "Got plenty of NCOs around here."

"I know."

"What's been going on around here?"

"I don't know. I just go out on the searchlight to different hills and OPs every night. But no NVA shooting like at Tiger Mountain, you know," chuckled Figuero.

Shaw grinned as he slowly stepped toward the mess hall. "You gotta work tonight?"

"Yes. I work tonight. Going back to sleep after I eat. You going to work?"

"Not tonight. And I need the sleep. Only got three hours last night. We had a firefight where I just left."

The morning sun was bright when Shaw woke up. Quickly flipping his wrist and bringing the watch close to his eyes, he realized that he had slept twelve sound hours. At the side of his bunk his feet pushed open the mosquito net that enclosed it. Then he got out. Stepping to the foot of his bunk, he stopped, reached down and lifted his prescription lens sunglasses from the top of the foot locker. After he squared them on his face he slipped on his trousers. It was the first time in several weeks that he had slept without trousers. He knew it was a luxury that had contributed to the soundness of his sleep.

Shaw grabbed his rifle after he laced his boots. He walked to the mess hall. He got down on toast, scrambled eggs, sausage, hotcakes, and orange juice. And his 157 pound frame required him to have another helping. He gulped the second helping in five minutes, a minute longer than the first. He was used to eating this way. He had acquired it at Firebase Mary Ann, where there always seemed to be an alert or other reason to man your post during mealtime.

Vietnamese women worked in base camp. Some worked in the mess halls as dishwashers. Others worked as maids and laundresses. The younger and prettier women did the maid and laundry work. They were the hoochgirls. Inside the searchlight unit a hoochgirl was washing clothes as Shaw walked back from breakfast. Her black satin pants were rolled to her knees. Her legs were taut. She stood in a tub of water, agitating the sudsy water with her feet.

Shaw stopped within a few feet of the hoochgirl and spoke while admiring her big, green eyes. "Will you wash my clothes?" He had washed everything by hand out in the field. It wasn't easy work.

The hoochgirl, wearing a wide-coned, straw hat, said, "It cost you 1 MPC for one uniform and one underclothes. I iron it, too." Her teeth were exceptionally white.

"I have four sets."

"No sweat, soul. You bring them."

Shaw's keen ears noted her voice was pitched quite high, yet soft, and clear. Maybe she can sing, he thought. Then he said, "I'll bring them back in a minute."

"You get high, soul?" she asked in a whisper. She reached in her lower blouse pocket and halfway pulled out a pack of marijuana cigarettes. Five were wrapped in a cellophane packet. "5 MPC."

Hell of a bargain Look how fat they're rolled, and I know it's dynamite herb. Everything that grows over here is! But Shaw had no intentions of smoking it. He knew that in the States the herb would easily sell for five times as much. Especially after he'd let a potential buyer take a puff. And he also knew if he cut it with some tobacco, he could increase his profits even more.

But since Shaw didn't know the young woman yet, he played it off. "Not now. I'll let you know if I decide later." It could have been a set-up as far as he knew.

"You go get clothes. I wash them today."

"Okay."

"Come on, man," a soldier rushing out of the transit barrack told Shaw. A second later the door slammed in front of Shaw.

Shaw sat comfortably on his foot locker while he

read the last two pages of the Baldwin paperback. Then he stood up, looked out the screen window and wondered why there was a formation at 0900. But then he realized he was in a place, platoon base camp in Da Nang, that probably was petty as the States. He wouldn't be surprised if they had roll call. Unhurriedly, he stepped out of the door and fell into formation. Being the last man, he was at the end. He glanced to the right and guessed there were twenty-five to thirty men. He saw mostly spec 4s. But when he saw only one of the six black soldiers was a spec 4, he thought angrily, what is this shit! Reading Baldwin's Southern play, *Blues for Mister Charlie,* had awakened and aroused his racial consciousness.

Lieutenant Green stepped from the orderly room. He walked proud, his head high. A stocky, black sergeant first class, his namestrip reading Digger, followed Green. The position of his head as he walked contrasted with the lieutenant's. It was almost as if he knew he wasn't supposed to be as proud as the white officer.

Before anyone in the rank could say attention, Green barked, "As you are, men." Then he stopped sharply, twelve feet in front of the center man.

The sergeant first class came to a dead stop at Green's side.

Green began. "For you men here from other platoons waiting to go on R&R, I'm 1st Lieutenant Green, the platoon leader here." He focused his blue eyes on a man to his right and said, "Tell me what day this is?"

"Independence day, sir."

"Since there's no independence here," Green returned, "I rather say July 4th. So this evening we're going to grill and barbecue as you would at home."

"YAY!" the rank sounded collectively and strongly.

"I ordered 10 slabs of ribs and 4 dozen steaks. Got potato salad, baked beans, cole slaw, and ice cream to go with it."

"Beautiful, sir!" someone commented.

"Well, eat your hearts out," Green ended.

Barbecued ribs and steaks. This place is something. A smile was on Shaw's face.

It was July 5th when Shaw awoke at ten hundred. He rose sluggishly from his bunk. The basketball playing and heavy eating of the previous evening had tired him almost as much as a full night of work would have. In his green underwear he reached for the glasses on his footlocker.

"Shaw!" a person to the back of the barrack blurted.

Thinking it was someone he knew from the States, Shaw tried to place the familiar voice before he put on his glasses and turned around. *Myers! From Cam Ranh.* He pivoted and put on his glasses. "Myers, my man!"

"Look at you brother Shaw. You ain't skinny no more." Myers was stepping toward Shaw. His strides were long. He was grinning, his gold tooth gleaming. As he stepped close to Shaw, he bent his elbows, his thick, dark forearms parallel to the floor, his palms up. "Give me some!"

Slap, sounded the palms when Shaw hit his down on Myers'.

They reversed the position of their palms and Myers enthusiastically returned the greeting.

"How long you been with the searchlights?" began Shaw.

"You know when you left Cam Ranh Bay?"

Shaw moved his head up and down.

"I left four days later."

"I didn't even know you was in artillery."

"Not field artillery. I was trained at Fort Bliss for air defense artillery—missiles, shit like that. What's the difference. It all flies."

Shaw laughed. "You still crazy." He paused. "You must have got in this morning?"

"Yeah. I was in the 4th platoon but got transferred here. I got in a little trouble in Chu Lai. Some crackers was fuckin with me. I had to cut three of 'em." Myers reached in his front pocket. A split second later he pulled out a 4 inch thin-shaped knife. He flipped his wrist and the blade popped out.

"How'd it happen?"

Myers closed the knife and put it back in his pocket. "I cut the chow line to get with my boy, Dixon. Then some big o' cracker walked up and grabbed me by the shoulder, saying I wasn't going to get in front of him. I told him I'd go on to the end of the line and then asked him nicely to take his hands off my shoulder. By then two more crackers crowded around. The big one, a spec 4, was still holding my shoulder, talkin about you darkies think you can just bogard on anything. So that's when I went for my shit. I came out swinging. Got all three across the hand or arm. They backed up."

"Didn't they have rifles?"

"Naw. Officers had to lock up the rifles. Mothafuckers in that infantry unit down there's crazy. They were shooting each other and shit." Myers paused briefly, then continued. "So one redneck cracker ran back and got the XO. The XO called the MPs, and they locked me up for a couple of days. So here I am. A Sergeant named Kennedy said it was for my own good that he transferred me. He said he heard some rumors about they was going to try and frag me."

"Kennedy! Stocky dude?"

"Yeah."

"He's cool, man! Me and him did a lot of time out in the bush together."

Nonchalantly Myers spoke. "Yeah. He's all right for a cracker."

Shaw lifted his trousers from the foot locker, began putting them on, then said, "Let me finish dressing, and I'll show you around. Then we can go eat."

"Solid."

After lunch Shaw went to the orderly room to pick up a letter that he was told the mail clerk overlooked during mail call.

Stepping out of the orderly room and heading for the day room to play pool, Shaw tore open the envelope. He pulled out the letter, and instantly a smile lit his face. The letter was from his brother.

Dear Jimmy,

I hope you're in good spirits and the best of health. Mom brought me a brand new pair of tennis shoes with some of the money you sent home to help. Thanks. Most of it she put in the bank along with the other money you told her to save for you.

I guess I might as well tell you. Tony, the one you used to play in the band with. He got killed trying to rob a bank. No other bad news.

I gave Sandra your address. She said she might write.

Another thing, there's a big market here for Vietnam reefer. It's supposed to be the best. A lot of guys bringing and sending it home. If you can sneak me some home in a package, I'll sell it for a commission.

Truly,
Joey

The last paragraph really touched Shaw. He gritted his teeth, knowing he wouldn't allow himself to get Joey involved with selling or smoking marijuana. He knew if he did, then next Joey would be pushing hard stuff and probably get hurt or locked up. He just wouldn't allow it. And he was determined to write Joey and tell him.

Then he thought if he wouldn't allow Joey to push marijuana, why should he push it himself? Right then he decided against taking any marijuana home.

Now a few steps from the dayroom, Shaw folded the letter and stuck it in his upper shirt pocket. He stepped up and then into the day room. A pool table took up a third of the room, a ping pong table another third, and a bar and some folding chairs filled the far end.

A black soldier with a very close hair cut was eyeing the cue ball. A second later he aimed the pool stick. He drew it back, then poked it forward, hitting the cue ball which in turn smacked the eight ball into the cross side pocket. The soldier looked up, smiled and winked one of his light brown eyes at Shaw, who was the only other person in the room.

"Wanna shoot a game?" asked Shaw as he waited on Myers to show.

"That's what I'm here for, bro." The soldier, a PFC, removed the balls from the pockets and racked them. "You can have the break," he said, eyeing Shaw. "You going on R&R?"

"Not yet. We're just waiting on a new searchlight to come down. The gooks blew the other one up."

"How'd that happen?" Excitement was in the soldier's voice.

Shaw broke as he began to tell the soldier, Greenwood, about the adventure.

Ten minutes later they finished the game, and Shaw had told him the story.

"How long you been in the country?" questioned Shaw.

"Nine, maybe ten weeks. Been assigned here except the first few days."

"How come you didn't get promoted with Figuero and the others?"

Increasing the volume of his voice, Greenwood answered, "Figuero got recommended by that Uncle

Tom, Sergeant Digger. I don't think he digs brothers—the black bastard; he sends most of them to the field. I'm in commo. Probably the only reason he ain't sent me. Only time I go out is to stand guard duty in that open field in the back of the compound."

Greenwood paused and touched his virtually bald head. "I'm going to tell you how Digger is. I let my wig grow. It looked good, man, Pretty decent length, too; I seen some brothers coming out of the field, going on R&R with their wigs twice as long."

Greenwood's voice went high pitched as he attempted to imitate Digger's. "PFC Greenwood, don't you know it doesn't look soldierly to wear your hair that long?"

Greenwood's voice went back to normal. It was very low pitched. "Sergeant, just because you're ashamed of your culture, doesn't mean I am. James Brown says, 'Say It Loud, I'm Black and I'm Proud'!" Greenwood took a breath. "That made him mad."

Greenwood's voice went high pitched again. "You gonna be a private if I see you with it like that tomorrow."

Greenwood spoke normally as he told Shaw what he did. "I just cut all my shit off. Then he had nerve enough the next day to tell me I didn't have to get it all cut off. Digger ain't shit, man!"

"Sho' don't sound like it. Where you from, anyway, brother?"

"Motown. You?"

"Naptown."

Shaw went out on a searchlight that night. His comrade was a spec 4 with four months left in the country.

They worked a bridge on the outskirts of Da Nang. The enemy never reared its face all night.

When he came in from the bridge at 0600 in the morning, he stayed up for breakfast. As he walked back to his barrack from the mess hall, he crossed paths with the hoochgirl who had washed his clothes. They talked, and she tried to get him to buy some marijuana.

"No," he said in a polite manner.

"You don't like me, soul?" she asked, disappointment in her voice. "Other soul brothers buy marijuana from me. Try to talk to me and tip me."

"I don't smoke the stuff! And you selling sex, too?"

"Sex?" A bewildered look etched her face.

"You boom-boom," he clarified.

The young lady smiled. "I have no reason."

"And I don't have any reason to get high!"

"Soul. I think you no like me. I like you." She reached out and moved her fingers across the namestrip of Shaw's uniform. "You say your name how?"

He spoke gently. "Shaw. What's yours?"

"I'm Pham."

He reached and stroked her black hair. She was 5' 1", and her hair fell down to her hips. He had always thought that she looked good. "Your hair is pretty," he mentioned, his eyes admiring it.

Her yellow cheeks went red as she blushed.

"How old are you?" asked Shaw.

"Me?" she said, seemingly surprised. "I'm eighteen."

"At least you're old enough for me to rap to," he said, probing.

"I no understand what you mean."

"Never mind."

She stared at his dark glasses, her eyes full of curiousity. "You are mys-mysterious."

"Naw I'm not." He took off his glasses.

Their eyes met for a moment and then Shaw heard his rank and name called. He turned around and saw Sergeant First Class Digger. Digger was not a tall man. However, at 195 pounds, he was a big man, and neither young nor old at 37. His skin was dark and oily, cleanly shaved. His hair was clipped very short around the sides of his fatigue cap. His lips, pink and full, contrasted with his angular nose, denying him full negroid features.

"I didn't mean to interrupt you," said the sergeant, grinning.

Why did you? You see me talking to this pretty little girl.

Digger continued, "I just wanted to get acquainted with you. This is a small unit. I kinda want to know everybody personally. I see you're a US. You got plans of staying in any longer than two?"

"None," Shaw said bluntly. "I just want to get out and go back to school."

Pham eased away.

"To get your GED?" asked Digger.

"Naw, bachelor's degree is music or engineering."

The sergeant's eyebrows raised. "Is that right?"

"Yeah."

"Well, I guess you don't need the Army. You young colored guys have opportunities I never had, which is why I chose to stay in the Army. I'll admit, I've had some tough times. But I just kept quiet and let things work themselves out. Young colored guys today want to protest, tell the white commander he's a racist to his face. It looks and sounds bad. My wife is German, and I want her to be proud of the colored serviceman."

"But if somebody's doing you wrong, how can you get satisfaction if you don't speak up?"

The sergeant didn't reply immediately. After a moment he stated, "Like I said, things 'll work themselves out. In the Army you take orders."

Forgetting he was speaking with an elder and superior, Shaw exclaimed, "Come on, man! Where you been!"

The sergeant stared Shaw in the eye, a frown on his dark face. "You're cocky, Shaw. Let me tell you the only way to make it in this unit is don't make waves. See you around." Sergeant Digger pivoted and walked away.

Crazy old man.

Shaw turned in a circle, trying to spot Pham. He saw her nowhere. *Well, I guess Digger blew that for me.*

It never occurred to him that Digger was the one he might have blown it with.

Shaw went back to his barrack. There, he slept until 1650. When he woke up, he walked to the shower stall. The burners had been aflame for fifteen minutes. He showered and shaved. Then he went back to the barrack and fitted himself into one of the uniforms Pham had laundered.

Myers was in the barrack. They left together, heading for the mess hall. "Have you been on R&R yet?" began Shaw.

"It's kind of early for when we got over here. But when I go, I'm going to Hong Kong. Gonna get me some nice threads made. Half dozen at least. Gonna be a clean mothafucker when I get back home."

"I'll probably go to Bangkok or Singapore. I hear

there's some nice sights, and some women as dark as sisters!"

"If I go first, I'll hip you to Hong Kong and bring some pictures back. You might change your mind."

"I might," grinned Shaw.

When they reached the mess hall, they entered and ate. They also talked about the outposts they would be going to that night.

Three days passed, the routine staying the same for Shaw. Still, he liked platoon base camp. It was more secure, making him more at ease. The PX was at his disposal daily. There were three hot meals each day. The showers were hot, and the large tanks provided much more water pressure than the 55 gallon barrels in the field. And there was recreation: ping pong, basketball, and pool. There were movies.

And there was Pham. He was positive that he was making progress with her. She always smiled, showing her well-kept teeth when she saw him. She always carried on a lengthy conversation with him, and sometimes the conversations got intimate.

One morning after breakfast Shaw saw Pham. She was hysterical. "Shaw, Shaw," she cried, running to him, tears rolling down her smooth cheeks.

"What is it?" he reacted, a deep frown on his face. He feared that she may have lost a member of her family in one of the Viet Cong attacks in the village last night.

"My money! All my money! It's no good! I saved lots of it."

"Did somebody steal it?"

"No. No. Will you help me?"

With a puzzled expression he said, "If I can."

She reached down in her brassiere and pulled out a roll of MPCs. She unfolded them and started counting.

Shaw's eyes widened under his dark glasses. He saw nothing but twenties, perhaps forty of them. More money than he had made since being in the country, he guessed.

She handed the money to him. "You change to new MPC for me?"

Then it dawned on Shaw what she was talking about. He had heard a rumor that the American military was going to exchange the MPC of all American servicemen. This would make the old MPC worthless once the ubiquitous exchange was made. It was a move, for one, to take the MPC out of the hands of Vietnamese. The Vietnamese government was in favor of this; it would increase the value of the piaster, thus keeping it the money standard of Vietnam by forcing the citizens to be leary of the MPC. Shaw had also heard a rumor that the upper echelon government officials had tipped off the clandestine move two days ago by all at once cashing in their MPCs for piasters.

"No problem," said Shaw, quickly stashing the roll of money in his pocket. He didn't want anyone to see the young woman give him the money. He looked at her and smiled. "And what do I get?"

"You want money? You take ten percent."

"Naw. I don't want any of your money."

Pham smiled for the first time during the conversation. "I know you want me like the other GIs."

Shaw didn't want to admit it, especially after she indicated the other soldiers wanted her too. He didn't want it to go to her head that she was so desirable.

"No," he said, turning away so that she couldn't read the lie on his face.

"I want you, Shaw. I like you very much," she said quietly.

Shaw could feel his heart thump. And for once in Vietnam it wasn't because he was scared or winded.

It was 1100 when Shaw checked his wristwatch. An order had come down one hour ago, stating that nobody would be allowed to leave the compound until noon. It also stated that anyone who had MPC was to get in line in front of the orderly room and have it exchanged for the new MPC.

"Next," said Sergeant Blake as he stuck his head out of the orderly room door.

Shaw was in front of the line now. He stepped up and into the orderly room. In the first office Lieutenant Green sat behind the desk, and Sergeant Digger sat at the side. Stacks of new MPC were in place on the desk.

"Have you got any money in the safe, Jimmy," asked Blake, standing in the doorway.

"I got it all on me, sarge." As Shaw stood in front of the desk, he reached in his pocket and pulled out the wad of twenties. Counting by twenty he laid each bill on the desk. Seven hundred forty dollars he counted out. Then he went in his wallet and pulled out some ones, fives and tens. He counted out an additional thirty-four dollars.

Digger, with his dark brown eyes, gave Shaw a resentful stare. "You pimpin or something?" Quickly, he grinned.

"Just saving it up for R&R, Sergeant Digger."

"How come you don't keep it in the safe?" returned

Digger. "I'd sure hate to see somebody steal it from you."

"I can take care of my money," snapped Shaw.

"You sure it's yours?" added Digger, looking at the lieutenant out of the corner of his eye.

Shaw spoke sassily. "I got it." However, beads of sweat jumped out on his forehead.

The lieutenant, ignoring the conversation between Digger and Shaw, counted out $774 in new MPC. He handed it to Shaw and said, "Be sure it's right before you leave."

"I counted it with you, sir. Thanks." Shaw turned and stepped out of the office. He went to lunch shortly thereafter.

After lunch Shaw met with Pham in a secluded section of the compound, a field tall with green shrubbery. There, he gave her $740. She tucked it away, then laid down a pink blanket. And on it she gave him what they both wanted.

"Shaw, wake up," a regular sergeant was saying in a moderate volume. He stood over Shaw's bunk.

Shaw, easily awakened, batted open his eyes. He placed his gaze on the soldier. The soldier was standing close enough for Shaw's naked eyes to clearly focus on him. It was the lieutenant's driver, Sergeant Crawford, the lanky, auburn head fellow from Seattle.

Shaw yawned. "Want me, sarge?"

"It's no hurry, but the lieutenant wants to see you before he leaves his office at five."

"What time is it now?" Shaw had his wristwatch and wallet under the pillow.

"Two minutes after four," returned the sergeant, glancing at his wristwatch.

"Okay. I'll be over there in about ten minutes."

At 1650 Shaw stepped into the doorway of the lieutenant's office and said, "PFC Shaw reporting, sir." He saluted when the lieutenant looked up.

Green returned the salute and said, "Come on in Shaw."

PFC Shaw moved forward and stopped just in front of the desk. He figured it wouldn't take long since the lieutenant didn't offer him a seat.

"We've got some new searchlight jeeps in. I'm going to send you out in the field with one at Firebase Helen."

"Am I going back out with McHale, sir?"

"No. He's staying here."

Since he was leaving and McHale staying, Shaw figured Digger set it up. He thought about what Greenwood had said. But then, he wanted to tell Lieutenant Green something, anyway. "Sir, I don't think I've been treated fairly. You've got men who've never been out in the field. I was out there three-and-a-half months straight. And I've only been in base camp a week." He paused, expecting Green to make a comment. He continued when Green didn't. "And you got men who've been in the country two months and they're spec 4s. Sir, I want to see the CO."

"Wait just one minute," the lieutenant said loudly. His face was red with anger. "Nobody goes over my head. And I promote my men by qualifications not seniority."

"Yes sir, but I feel being out in the field for three-and-a-half months on searchlight almost every night has made me know more about it than those two month base camp men. They don't see much action or go out every night."

The lieutenant veered from the issue. "I understand your attitude leaves something to be desired?"

"It probably does now," Shaw admitted. "But you couldn't say that when I first came here."

"I'll tell you what Shaw, since you seem not to really want to go back in the field right away, I'll keep you assigned here for a few weeks longer. I like your idea of letting some of the new men work in the field."

Shaw kept his joy contained; he stood straight-faced. "I'm glad you liked the suggestion, sir," he added. Then he pivoted and quickly stepped out of the door, not wanting to give the lieutenant a chance to renege in person. He was surprised the lieutenant gave in so quickly.

The rising sun cast a tangerine hue in the Eastern sky. Spec 4 Dean and PFC Shaw had just returned to base camp from an outing at Hill 265, on the outskirt of Da Nang. As Shaw took his pack and flak jacket into the barrack, he saw Sergeant First Class Digger opening the doors to the barracks and looking inside them. When Shaw stepped back outside, Digger was with Dean.

"Good morning, PFC Shaw," said Digger.

Shaw returned the greeting.

Digger's eyes moved down to a smoke grenade attached to Shaw's shirt. The grenade was round and plastic, not oval and steel like a fragmentation grenade, nor was it explosive. The grenade had been given to

Shaw by Marine Lance Corporal Jones. For that reason alone it carried sentiment. And Shaw knew, too, the grenade might have to be used for a cover screen. Digger spoke. "You know you can't carry grenades around base camp. Are you going to check it in the arms room?"

"You've seen it before. It's only a smoke grenade," defended Shaw.

"I don't care. Check it in."

Dean, the gray-eyed, blond-haired soul brother, laughed and turned toward Shaw. "You'd better check it in. If somebody throws a smoke grenade at him, he can't blame it on you."

Still looking at Digger, Shaw concealed his anger and calmly said, "No sweat. Just as soon as it opens."

Digger stepped away and checked inside another barrack.

"I like the way you handled that," said Dean.

"Fuck Digger!" Shaw truly expressed.

Shaw was enjoying his stay in Da Nang. He had been there a month. Now August, he had scheduled his three day R&R. He decided on Hong Kong. Myers had come back the last day of July, boasting about how slick it was. He had showed Shaw some Polaroid pictures of some interesting scenery and pretty women. Now that Shaw had fallen out with Pham, he was ready to meet some of the young ladies in the pictures.

He and Pham had broken up a week ago. It had happened when she seriously insisted on him taking her to America when he finished his tour. She indicated there was nothing for her to look forward to in her country with it at war all the time. She said she wanted to go to America and be a dental hygienist like a friend of hers who had left with a GI. Shaw told her then that he wouldn't take her back because he didn't want to be tied down just yet, and that it wouldn't be easy for her to make it in the States by herself. She became upset and told him that she didn't want to talk to him anymore. And she hadn't.

Off for the night because he would be flying to Hong Kong early the next morning, Shaw was sitting in the dayroom playing poker. Chips gave the game a more respectable look. The other men sitting at the table were Myers, Greenwood, and Sims. Sims was a black spec 4 from Jacksonville, Florida. He was the Army cook assigned to the Marine mess hall.

The men had been playing for two hours. It was now 2200.

Myers spoke as he conceded defeat. "You too tough for me, brother Sims." He had just lost a big pot to Sims. Myers swept his three remaining red chips off the table and into his hand, gave them to Greenwood, then stood up.

Greenwood pitched the chips into a small box on the table and then went in his front pocket. He pulled out a roll of ones and peeled off three. "Here," he said, handing the money to Myers. "Maybe you'll have better luck next time."

"I'm retiring from gambling," insisted Myers. He sounded discouraged. "I cain't never win." He turned and faced Shaw. "What you gonna do?"

"I guess I better give it up now and leave with you," he answered. But he looked at Charlie Greenwood and Ray Sims. "The way Ray's going, he might break into some of this R&R money. And I don't want that to happen."

"I'll have to win a whole lot of what you done already won," said Sims, grinning.

Shaw raked in an armful of chips and started handing them to Greenwood one by one.

"Y'all niggers done won all the money," Greenwood said sassily, shifting his light brown eyes from Shaw to Sims.

"Count my money and stop jivin nigga," Shaw said in humor.

Greenwood had put all the chips into the box. He reached in his pocket and pulled out a wad of ones and fives. He counted out $52, folded the money, then flipped it to Shaw.

Impatiently Myers said, "Let's go!"

"Be cool, I'm coming," said Shaw, pulling out the $200 R&R money, wrapping the other money around it. Shaw rose calmly, pulling out his wallet, securing his money in it. Then he stepped out the door with Myers.

In minutes Myers and Shaw reached the barrack. Since they hadn't been permanently assigned to base camp, their bunks were still in the transit barrack. As Myers stepped inside, he switched on the lights. The two other men lying inside momentarily raised their heads. Shaw, following Myers in, said, "We don't need the lights." Myers switched them off. Both men went to their areas, undressed and fell in the bunks.

It was late, and the door to the transit barrack squeaked. Shaw's bunk was closest to the door. He normally slept lightly. When the door squeaked, he was awakened. He figured a man was coming in from searchlight duty. He opened his eyes wide for a moment and saw the figure of a man outside the door. Without his glasses he couldn't make out who it was. As he closed his eyes again, it dawned on him that the person *was leaving*. Opening his eyes, he lifted his pillow and pulled out his watch. He read the time—0375. Suddenly he felt his heart throb. Again, he reached under his pillow, and he frantically fumbled around underneath it. And, as he had feared, no billford. *Hold it!* He said to himself. *I forgot to put my billfold under my pillow last night. I left it in my pants!* He jumped up and in two long strides was at the foot of his bunk, where his foot locker sat. He took his sunglasses from the foot locker and quickly squared them on his face. Then nervously he felt the rear of his pants as they laid on the locker. The rear pockets were as flat as a newly made bunk. His mouth instantly became dry. His eyelids twitched as he held back the tears of anger. How could he let this happen? he thought. The drill sergeants had always stressed lock up all valuables in the safe or sleep with them under you.

Then like a jackrabbit Shaw shot out the door, no pants on, trying to locate the soldier or Marine who had just left the barrack. He circled the barrack, and not able to spot anyone he came back inside. He dressed and looked at his rifle. At the last moment he decided against taking the weapon. After pulling the trigger on the enemy he knew that he might do the same if he found the thief. Really, he felt that he would much rather beat the hell out of him, regardless of his size.

Ready to play Sherlock Holmes, Shaw thought about a suspect. The first person to come to mind was Myers. But he was very reluctant to believe it was him. He knew Myers had the boldness to be a rogue, but he figured Myers wouldn't be so cold as to steal from a close partner. Shaw felt like their partnership had grown so that it was like a brotherhood. Nevertheless he turned deliberately toward Myers bunk. To Shaw's great satisfaction Myers was stretched out like a dead man. Then suddenly, it occurred to him that Greenwood was the prime suspect. For one, he was up working in the commo bunker.

Shaw rushed out of the barrack. The screen door slammed behind him. He stepped quickly across the U-shaped unit. When he reached the commo bunker, he entered it by snatching open the wooden door.

Greenwood and a specialist 5th class spun in their seats and looked at Shaw with widened eyes.

"What's the deal with you, storming in here like that this time of the morning, PFC?" asked the specialist, holding up his short, pointed nose.

"Yeah, Shaw?" Greenwood coolly added. "I thought you was a gook at first. I got ready to grab my rifle."

"Have you been out of this bunker lately?" inquired Shaw in an alienating tone. He gave Greenwood a serious stare.

"Naw! What's wrong with you, man?"

Shaw gave no reply. He turned toward the specialist, Berg, and asked, "Has he?"

The dark haired, olive eyed Berg sharply replied, "He said no. And before you ask, neither have I. What the fuck's going on!"

"I got beat for my billford and R&R money."

"What!" said Greenwood. "And you thought I did it? Come on, brother. I'm another brother, a true one," he voiced in disgust.

"All I figure is it was somebody I was playing cards with."

"Word gets around, Shaw," said Berg. "I heard you won about fifty, myself. It doesn't have to be one of them."

"Maybe you're right," said Shaw, less emotional, yet his heart raced. "Still, I'm gonna check out Sims."

Shaw gently opened the screen door to the barrack where Sims was bedding. When he saw Sims lying motionlessly on the bunk, he began to think it was someone other than the guys he had been in the dayroom playing cards with. He really didn't want to believe that a brother had beat him, anyway. He had been impressed by the close ties the brothers had formed, particularly out in the field. Shaw eased his head back out of the door. Then he let the door close as if a crying baby had just fallen asleep.

Shaw brought his forearm up and looked at his wristwatch. Seeing that only ten minutes had elapsed from the time the theft occurred, he decided to keep looking. Swiftly he walked around the Army unit, then the two adjacent Marine units, looking for any suspicious person or for anybody. All he saw were bunker guards, seemingly confined to their posts. He decided all he could do now was go back to his bunk and try and get some sleep.

Shaw was awakened at 0725. The heavy hands of Sergeant Digger were shaking the foot rail of his bunk. For a moment Shaw was relieved to think the incident was but a dream.

"So you let somebody steal your money," Digger began.

Shaw's heart sank.

"Have you got any idea who it was?" Digger returned.

"Naw. All I saw was a figure in the dark, medium built and height."

"Was it a colored guy or white guy?" Digger asked in a soft voice.

"I couldn't tell."

"Well, I'm having a shake down at this moment. I don't know if it's going to do any good. The guy's done probably hid the money. By the way, Sergeant Crawford heard about what happened and he told me to tell you that he'd loan you the money if you still wanted to go on R&R."

"Crawford? Tell him thanks. But I'm too upset at myself. I wouldn't have a good time. Maybe I'll reschedule it in a couple of months. I'll have saved some more money by then, too."

It was shortly after 0800 as Shaw and Myers sat in a full mess hall, eating and talking. "What was you thinking last night, not putting up your money?" asked Myers.

"I don't know, said Shaw, shaking his head in disgust. "Drinking that little beer laid me out." Shaw picked at his food, barely eating.

Greenwood joined the two at the table. Sitting himself and his tray down, he clenched his fist and shook it at Shaw as if to say *keep the faith*. "What's happening, y'all?" he opened.

"Not much," said Shaw and Myers, one after another.

Greenwood leaned toward Shaw and whispered, "I

believe Sims got your money, man. I should have told you last night that I trimmed him for every dollar. We shot craps when y'all left. He's a funny acting brother, anyway. Real sneaky."

"I don't have any proof, man. I don't want to accuse anybody like I did you last night unless I got something solid to go on." Shaw paused as he thought back to something that had appeared strange. "I don't have to work again tonight. I'm going to find out something."

At 2300 most of the soldiers in the searchlight unit were sleeping, even though flares and gunfire burst far in the distance. Shaw had his rifle in hand as he tiptoed to Sims' barrack. Easing the door open, he looked inside. Sims laid still in his bunk. The night was hot like the night before—in the mid nineties. This time, however, Sims slept in his underwear. That convinced Shaw that Sims was the thief. The night before Sims laid with his pants on. Shaw stepped lightly toward Sims' bunk, careful not to awake anyone. At the bunk Shaw placed the cold, black, steel barrel to the man's temple. Sims woke immediately, looking at Shaw as he saw a black devil.

"Where's my money, mothafucker!" Shaw whispered fiercely. He looked as furious as a man who had just been spit upon.

"I didn't steal it!" Sims exclaimed, trembling.

Shaw figured he had frightened him too much, assuming a man frightened for his life would always lie to preserve it. "Okay, Sims, I cain't prove it. But I'm almost sure you did it. If I ever catch you stealing from me or any other brother, your ass is mine!"

The soldier in the next bunk rolled over toward the commotion.

Shaw heard him and quickly pulled his weapon away from Sims. He turned and walked out the barrack, knowing Sims would never admit to having stolen the money or return it.

At 0850 the next morning the Army platoon stood in formation. The formation had been called by Platoon Sergeant Blake who had yelled in every barrack before breakfast. Shaw was concerned that Sims might have told Blake about last night's incident with the rifle. But it was his word against Sims, Shaw thought, since nobody else fully saw what had happened.

When Shaw saw the lieutenant step out of the NCO and officer barrack with a helmet and flak jacket on, he knew the matter was more serious than what he had thought.

"Stay at ease, men," Lieutenant Green said, approaching the rank. He stopped near the center of the rank and continued, "As of zero-six hundred this morning most of Da Nang has been on red alert. Charlie struck almost everywhere last night. He even blew up some planes. Now he has a foothold in the city and may launch a drive on our military units from there. So I advise you against leaving the compound until the alert is lifted. And it would be a good idea to wear your helmet and flak jacket, even in this heat. I grant you a piece of shrapnel is hotter."

A few of the men in the rank laughed.

The platoon leader continued, "Check your weapons and ammunition. Intelligence says the enemy is in a position to strike harder tonight. I'm going to keep as many men as I can at base camp tonight. We have a lot of perimeter to defend if it comes to that. You're dismissed."

The rank broke instantly, amidst a buzz of conversation.

Shaw and Myers stepped into their barrack, talking of cleaning their rifles.

When darkness fell across Da Nang, searchlight beaconed into the sky and flares shot skyward. And what appeared as red streamers coming from the sky, was Puff the Magic Dragon, an American aircraft, firing three multi-barrelled machine guns at an incredible rate of 18,000 rounds a minute, every fifth round a red tracer. Although this activity was happening miles from Freedom Hill, those soldiers and Marines at Freedom Hill were prepared if not anxious to do battle. Machine gun crews had stacked containers of ammunition in their nest. Three and four men, rather than two, manned guard bunkers. And the men who slept did so fully clothed and seemingly with one eye and ear open. Any close flash of light or closing intensity of arms fire unbunked them until the light or sound moved on.

It was 0128 as Shaw sat behind a double wall of sandbags with Myers and Dean. The area in front and around them was calm. At 0136 the first mortar whistled over their heads and exploded harmfully 150 feet from them. But it quickly dispelled the rumor that the enemy might not hit Freedom Hill.

Men scrambled out of barracks to their posts as eight more mortars exploded inside the compound. Three barracks were blown apart, and some men were too late in getting out of them.

Shaw, Myers, and Dean stayed down while the mortar rounds rained in. As soon as the incoming mortar rounds slackened, they raised their heads, knowing the enemy would be rushing through some blown opening in the perimeter wire. "Who's manning the machine guns?" asked Dean, breathing heavily. There were two machine guns, one at each end of the straight, 350 foot perimeter. The next line of defense was a number of sandbag barricades like the one Shaw, Myers, and Dean knelt behind.

"Somebody like Gladson or Figuero," answered Myers. "Don't know his ass from his face."

"I hope not," added Shaw. "I dig Fig and Gladson but I sure hope they're not on any one of them guns. They're key. How come bad-ass Digger didn't get on one?"

"Shit," returned Myers. "He ain't gonna risk his ass if he don't have to. Can you blame him?"

"Naw," said Shaw, tensing up as he heard a mortar round whistle very close over his head.

Doom! the mortar went a moment later, fifty feet from them.

Shaw turned around and saw a jeep fly into chunks. Rubber, glass, and steel were thrown twenty-five feet. He ducked, telling the others to do so, too.

Rat-ta-ta-ta...tat, sounded one of the M-60s.

A red flare burst high above the compound, indicating condition red—attack. And then a white flare burst open, lighting the compound and perimeter. The machine gunner had stopped the first two VC that tried to lay a mattress over the barbed wire concertina.

A series of mortars came whistling in. *Doom! Doom! Doom! Doom! Doom!,* they explosed one after another, falling in a straight line, moving sideward, just inside the perimeter.

Shaw knew that was the cover for the VC to climb over their dead comrades. He started firing his M-16 on automatic in the direction of the dead Viet Cong. But due to the smoke and dust the mortar rounds created, he couldn't see what he was hitting. But he could hear cries of agony.

Dean and Myers fired in that direction, too. When the dust and smoke cleared, seven more bodies were sprawled on top of the wire.

Boom! Boom!, explosions sounded.

Shaw and his comrades looked left. There, they saw a squad of VC rushing through the first opening in the concertina wire.

Firing AK-47s, the VC penetrated deep inside the perimeter. Thirty yards they had advanced despite heavy small arms fire. Bullets landed everywhere on the left side of the flare lit compound, but the VC had already overtaken the M-60 bunker on that side with a hand grenade.

With another series of explosions, Shaw turned his head to the center of the perimeter again. Viet Cong torsos, limbs and guts flew backward. They had tripped the wire that activated the claymore mines.

Shaw's heart was beating like a jackhammer from the excitement, but he never realized it. He did fear the VC might overrun the compound and kill everyone, including himself. And he knew that he and his unit had to fight like mad to prevent it.

Myers was trying to fling a hand grenade sixty-five

yards to the captured machine gun bunker when a couple of bullet rounds sounded close over his head. *Zip, zip!* His eyes widened. "Hey, man," he said, looking at Shaw, then Dean, "those rounds came from behind." It was the units third line of defense. "Those dudes cain't shoot."

Shaw heard his heart thump when he thought Sims might be behind him. Sweat popped onto his forehead. He was beginning to feel like he was in a vise: the enemy squeezing in from the front and another kind of enemy stationary in the back. "Stay low, y'all!" Shaw screamed. Rifle fire seemed to crackle everywhere as tracers and flares lit the compound like it was a midway. "I'm going to crawl over to the other machine gun. Whoever's over there's scared to use it or don't know how!"

"Take care of yourself, man!" voiced Myers.

Crawling away, Shaw warned, "Watch out for those rounds in the rear. They might be Sims' rifle. I threatened him last night."

"We will, and we'll cover you, too!" yelled Dean, perspiring profusely.

Shaw crawled with the ease of a snake and covered fifty yards within a minute. He stopped crawling and then laid flat on his belly ten yards from the bunker.

The battle to Shaw's left reached a stalemate. The VC couldn't advance, and American rifle fire and errant hand grenades couldn't wipe them from the captured machine gun bunker.

Shaw yelled toward the machine gun bunker on the right side of the compound. "It's PFC Shaw!" He wanted to alert the three or four men who should have been in the bunker so that they wouldn't mistake him for a gook.

No one answered.

"It's Shaw," he yelled again, removing the old magazine from his M-16, inserting a new one and then taking the safety off the deadly little rifle. He rose to a crouch and ran into the bunker, his rifle out front.

Inside the bunker he saw a bloody body slumped over the machine gun. He turned the body over and saw it was Greenwood, a bullethole in the forehead. He went into a momentary daze. Then he thought the others must have chickened out and ran. With adrenaline now flowing in quantity, he went into a rage as he threw Greenwood's heavy body off the weapon. Grabbing the 60, he aimed it toward the other machine gun bunker and pulled the trigger. The weapon shook his upper body vigorously, but he held his aim steady, pouring a heavy stream of bullets and tracers into the target. Less than a minute later he loaded the M-60 with another belt of ammo. But now rifle rounds zinged into the bunker he was in. Disregarding them, Shaw let loose with the 60 again, saturating the other bunker, flushing out several VC, who were then cut down by rifle fire.

Shaw stopped firing for a moment. Then through his peripheral vision he saw three black garmeted VC dash through a fresh opening in the perimeter wire. Quickly, he pivoted, bringing the machine gun in the same direction. He opened fire. *Rat-ta-ta-ta-tat!* He knocked them off their feet, but it was a fraction too late to prevent one from firing a RPG. *Zoom!*

A split second later the bunker burst like an over inflated inner tube.

Shaw felt no pain. Shaw felt nothing.

Epilogue

It was in the Army hospital in Japan when Shaw awoke from the coma. He had been in the coma eight days. He was in a hospital room by himself, he realized that. A flashback came to him. It was of the explosion, but he remembered nothing after that. With both hands he pulled the clean, white linen off him. He stared at his legs, seeing they were intact. He reached up and felt the gauze bandage around his head. He figured then that it was because of a concussion he may have received.

A while later two white coated Army medical captains stepped in the room. They turned with a smile and talked with each other as they noticed Shaw had come around.

Shaw tried to hear what they were saying. He couldn't. They were close enough, he thought. And their lips had the movement of audible conversation. Still, he could not hear them. For that matter, Shaw realized, he didn't hear any sounds. Then he realized nobody could come out of an explosion in one piece. He was glad that he was alive, he guessed. Tears dropped down his cheek when he thought about never playing the piano; what would be the use with no hearing to appreciate the music.

One of the doctors handed Shaw an envelope.

Shaw's weak fingers and poor coordination caused

him to fumble with it for a moment. Then slowly he tore it open and removed the contents. It read:

>Spec. 4 Ortho Myers
>8/11/68

Brother Shaw:

I thought I'd drop you this line before you go back to the states. First, I hope everything turns out okay as far as the injury. You didn't look too bad when I carried you out of that bunker, except being out.

Thought you'd want to know they promoted us to spec 4 a couple of days after the firefight. And you also got recommended for a silver star. You shouldn't have no problem getting it. Everybody in base camp knows you deserve it.

Keep in touch with me when you get back to the World!

And Pham said hi. She cried when she heard you got hurt.

>Your man,
>Brother Myers

A broad grin swept across Shaw's brown, unshaven face.

One of the doctors jotted something on a piece of paper and handed it to Shaw. It stated: Why are you crying and smiling?

After Shaw read it he eyed the bespeckled doctor and spoke. "My hearing is gone is the reason I was crying." He noted it was very strange not being able to hear himself talk. "And the beautiful letter my partner sent is why I'm smiling."

The doctor took a minute to write something on his

pad. Then he tore the paper off the pad and gave it to Shaw.

Shaw read it: *Just smile now. You're going home and receive the best care available. Also, your hearing loss is only temporary. With the proper treatment your hearing will return in two or three weeks. Both your eardrums were bursted. Though bad, not damaging enough to make it permanent.*

The smile on Shaw's face widened immensely, but a moment later he wanted to cry again, remembering vividly the miseries and inhumanities of war, and knowing Pham, Myers, and a whole lot of others still had to deal with it.

ABOUT THE AUTHOR

Johnny Carn's interest in creative writing started in grade school, where a crafty teacher had the class sketch stories about the things they liked most.

He has resided in Indianapolis since birth, being raised on the West, North and East sides of town. He was born in 1947.

By trade he's an electronics technician. He got his formal training at IUPUI and IVY Tech through the GI bill. At IUPUI he also took several courses in literature and composition, inspiring him to begin *Shaw's Nam*.

He spent a year in Vietnam, serving with the U.S. Army as an enlisted man.

Besides creative writing Johnny Carn's other avocation is jazz music. He has promoted it, DJ-ed it, and spent countless hours listening to it. He is also an aspiring acoustic bassist who admits he may never find the time to master the difficult instrument like his idol and friend, Richard Davis.

Watch for the author's forthcoming novel *The AIC and Ms. Liary* (intrigue). It will be published in '85.

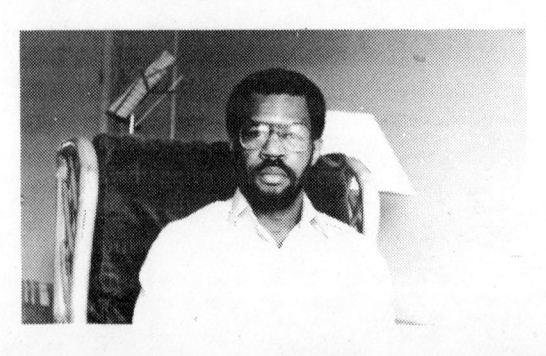